GUYS READ

HEROES & VILLAINS

Also available in the Guys Read Library of Great Reading

GUYS READ

HEROES & VILLAINS

EDITED AND WITH AN INTRODUCTION BY
JON SCIESZKA

STORIES BY

LAURIE HALSE ANDERSON, CATHY CAMPER AND RAÚL THE THIRD, SHARON CREECH, JACK GANTOS, CHRISTOPHER HEALY, DEBORAH HOPKINSON, INGRID LAW, PAM MUÑOZ RYAN, LEMONY SNICKET, AND EUGENE YELCHIN

WITH ILLUSTRATIONS BY
JEFF STOKELY

WALDEN POND PRESS
An Imprint of HarperCollinsPublishers

Walden Pond Press is an imprint of HarperCollins Publishers.
Walden Pond Press and the skipping stone logo are trademarks and registered
trademarks of Walden Media, LLC.

Library of Congress Control Number: 2016957939
ISBN 978-0-06-238561-1 (trade bdg.) — ISBN 978-0-06-238560-4 (pbk.)

Typography by Joel Tippie
17 18 19 20 21   CG/LSCH   10 9 8 7 6 5 4 3 2 1

First Edition

CONTENTS

BEFORE WE BEGIN . . .

I've always been interested in heroes. I remember wanting to be like the kid in *The Carrot Seed* who grows the giant carrot. I was pretty sure I could be as woodsman-amazing as Davy Crockett. I knew that one day I would be as good as Robin Hood, as helpful as Spider-Man, as cool as James Bond, and as crazy a fighter against injustice as my favorite hero of all—Bugs Bunny.

Though I was also always just as intrigued by villains. The Grinch was a guy I wanted to know more about. I liked the raucous pirate Long John Silver. I admired the Joker for his can-do spirit. And I thought the Evil Queen was way more exciting than Snow White.

But what makes a hero?

What makes a villain?

The dictionary says a hero is "a person admired for courage, outstanding achievements, or noble qualities." And that a villain is "a person who does mean, evil things on purpose."

But Guys Read thinks there is more to it than that.

So we asked a bunch of our favorite writers and a couple of our favorite illustrators to consider the question of heroes and villains. And man, did they come up with the wildest answers.

Inside this volume of the Guys Read Library of Great Reading, you will meet a kid whose drawings make him a hero, a villain who acts like a hero, a hero who becomes a villain and then a hero and then maybe not either.

You will discover heroic deeds that need to be done behind the sucking black-hole vacuum-vortex thing in the back of a locker.

You will decide if you would be a hero or a villain if your mother was arrested for murder.

You will meet a famous American Revolutionary War general who was both hero and villain . . . covered in pelican poop.

And check out the heroic-villainous cover and illustrations for all of this!

Okay, I may have said too much already.

Get in there, get reading, and decide for yourself—Hero? Villain? Or . . . ?

Jon Scieszka

THE VILLAIN'S GUIDE TO BEING A HERO
BY CHRISTOPHER HEALY

There was a time when the mere mention of the name Deeb Rauber would send people into shrieking fits; make them curl, weeping, under their beds; or cause them to swoon, face-first, into their half-eaten porridge. This was a time, obviously, when people were very melodramatic. But even so, they had good reason to fear Mr. Rauber, whom you may perhaps know better as the "Bandit King."

For years, the bards had been chronicling the diabolical exploits of the dreaded Bandit King. From his first pretzel robbery at the tender age of six to his brazen yeti heist at the slightly-less-tender age of twelve, Rauber's every devious stunt became fodder for nightmare-inducing bedtime stories. Though only on the brink of puberty, Deeb commanded an army of brutal thugs, stuffed his chambers to their ceilings with plundered treasure, and sat upon the throne of his very own, very dangerous kingdom: Rauberia. It was for these reasons and more that the Bandit King was not only the most infamous person in the Thirteen Kingdoms, but perhaps the most famous as well.

Until the League of Princes came along.

These days the League was the only thing the bards ever sang about. And why? A whole team full of Prince Charmings? That's not a band of heroes, that's the punchline to a lousy joke. And yet, ever since those goody-goodies from the tales of Snow White, Rapunzel, Cinderella, and Sleeping Beauty decided to team up and save a few kingdoms, people hadn't been paying nearly enough attention to Deeb anymore. At least that was the way Deeb saw it. When he snuck into Svenlandia's royal bedchamber and stole the spun-gold nightshirt right off the sleeping king, for instance, he expected to hear people yapping about it for days. But what was the big new bard song that week? "The League of Princes Defeat the Goblin Horde." And the week after that, did we have a hit tune called "The Bandit King Kidnaps the Hound of Carpagia"? No, it was "The League of Princes and the

Merfolk Rescue." Not even when Deeb trapped the entire Valerian royal family in a vat of molasses did he get a mention. And do you have any idea how difficult it is to get molasses out of royal velvet? No, that week the bards wrote "The League of Princes Help Three Goats Cross a Bridge." It was enough to make an evil genius consider throwing in his stolen towel.

"Today might be the day I call it quits, Vero," Deeb Rauber said, tossing his short, spindly legs over one arm of his heavy, oaken throne.

"And what is it you will be quitting?" replied the Bandit King's right-hand man of the moment. Vero was a tall, dashing swordsman with a thin mustache and a thick ponytail. He spoke in a heavy Carpagian accent. "The nose picking, I hope. It is, as we say in my country, *kind of gross.*"

"Villainy, Vero. I'm quitting villainy," Deeb snapped. He flicked a booger at the swordsman to emphasize his point. "What's the point of being evil if your presence can't make people sour their pantaloons?"

"There's always the free doughnuts," said another of Deeb's black-clad followers as he laid a tray of pilfered baked goods by the throne.

Deeb grabbed a cruller from the pile and licked off some powdered sugar. "Meh."

"This dreariness, sir—this cloud of blah that hovers over your head like a rich duke's big, poofy wig—it is not so inspirational for the men," Vero said.

Deeb glanced around the room at his brawny, stubble-chinned minions. Normally, they'd be joking, roughhousing, and candy-bingeing. But today, they were moping about like a bunch of gnomes who'd lost their pointy hats.

Deeb sighed. "It does seem like a waste to kick it in before I even grow hair on my chest." He took a bite of his cruller, wiped his hands on his leather vest, and bounced the uneaten portion of the pastry off the head of a nearby bandit. "I just need to pull off a job big enough to grab the people's attention away from those stinking princes and put it back on me where it belongs."

"I believe we have a few recently abducted visitors in our cells—fools who made the mistake of crossing the border into Rauberia," Vero said, tapping the hilt of his rapier. "Perhaps one of them will merit some sort of ransom?"

"I suppose. Well, parade 'em through here," Deeb said, forcing a smile. "At worst, we can run 'em through the wedgie machine. That's always good for a pick-me-up."

"Ah, there you go," said Vero. "It is nice to see a glimmer of the old, sociopathic gang leader I am used to."

The first unfortunate soul brought before the king was a

scrawny old man in a ragged shirt and peasant pants.

"A farmer?" Deeb asked, sounding bored already. "Well, that's useless. Ooh, unless you grow magic beans. You grow any magic beans?"

The old man shook his head apologetically. "Just eggplants."

"Next!" Deeb shouted.

The old man was dragged off and replaced before the throne by a tiny, sad-faced fellow in a dirty green suit. A beefy guard held the itty-bitty man up by his ankle.

"A leprechaun! Now we're talking!" Deeb popped upright. "Where's your gold, Leppy?"

"I haven't got any gold," the leprechaun grumbled. "Ye've already stolen all of it. I can see most of me treasure sittin' right there behind yer big bowl of licorice whips."

Deeb deflated. "Well, if you've got no gold, what good are you to me? Back to the dungeon!"

"Wait!" the desperate leprechaun called out. "I can do a jig for ye!"

Deeb rolled his eyes. "Dungeon."

"I can remove curses!" the leprechaun shouted. "Are there any curses ye want me to get rid of?"

"Get rid of curses? Why would I do that? I love curses. Wanna hear some of my favorites?" And as the leprechaun was carried off, the Bandit King treated him to a long list of unsavory words.

Vero, who sat on a treasure chest by the wall, furrowed his brow in concern. "Perhaps this next one will, as we say in my country, *do the trick.*"

The third and final prisoner was a portly bald man.

"All right, what's your story?" Deeb asked.

"I'm just a messenger, Your Bandit-ness," the man said. "I was on my way to deliver a letter. I didn't realize I'd trespassed on—"

"Save it, mailman. Hand over the note."

The messenger reluctantly placed the parchment into the Bandit King's sticky fingers. Deeb unfolded it, scanned it, and began chuckling. "Oh, this is rich." He stood on his throne and read: "'O, brave and noble League of Princes, the village of Fizzledorf is in dire need of your aid. For months we have been repeatedly set upon by a monstrous beast. The vicious creature has attacked townsfolk, destroyed homes, and devoured livestock. We fear it is only a matter of time before one of us becomes the monster's next midnight snack. Please, bold princes, we beseech you—only heroes of your caliber could best a beast so ferocious and save what is left of Fizzledorf.'"

The messenger cleared his throat. "So," he said. "As you

can see, I really do need to get that letter to the League as quickly as possible." He wiped the sweat from his brow. "If you'll kindly just pass it back—"

"Tell me what you know about this beast," Deeb said, hopping down and pacing a tight circle around the messenger, his nest of black hair tickling the man's nose as he passed.

"Um, it's big, like a bear," the man said. "Huge fangs and claws. Powerful. Can shred a wooden door like a piece of cheese. There are these siblings who live down the road from me; the beast completely flattened two out of their three houses."

Vero laughed. "Just as in that bard song about the trio of piggies, yes?"

"That's right!" The messenger nodded vigorously. "'The Tale of the Three Pigs.' The bards changed a bit, but that's pretty much the story of Fizzledorf."

Deeb stopped in front of the messenger and glared up into the man's eyes. "Um, didn't the wolf get boiled at the end of that story?" he said.

"Like I said, the bards got some details wrong," the man said. "And, um, I've seen wolves before, Your Bandit-ness. This creature is no ordinary wolf."

"You better not be lying to me, Bozworth," Deeb said.

"Know what we do to liars around here? Pants on fire. Literally."

Deeb sat down and stroked the beard he fully believed he'd have one day. He did so silently, and for quite some time. If the gears in the Bandit King's mind cranked slowly, it was probably because they were gummed up with obsessive thoughts of caramel and nougat. After several silent minutes, he jumped to his feet, thrusting a finger in the air. "I've got it! Gather 'round, men. I'm about to pull off the greatest heist in the history of thievery."

"Please, sir, do tell us," said Vero.

"I'm going to this Fizzledorf place, and I'm going to kill their monster," the Bandit King said, grinning wickedly.

"So . . . ," Vero began cautiously. "You are going to do something . . . helpful?"

"No!" Deeb scoffed. "I'm going to steal the glory from the League of Princes! I've been going about this all wrong. If the people want a song about heroics and bravery and all that nonsense, then that's just what they'll get. Only this one's gonna be starring me! You follow? What should have been the League's victory is going to be mine! I'll get all the credit! The Prince Charmings will be forgotten again as every bard in the Thirteen Kingdoms sings of the awesome power of the Bandit King!"

"This plan," Vero said. "It is . . . very interesting."

But Deeb didn't seem to notice his deputy's skepticism. He was too busy dancing in his piles of gold and shoving doughnut bits into his mouth.

The messenger made a little cough. "So, can I . . . go?"

"Oh, you're going all right, Bozworth," Deeb said. "*With me*, as my guide. Lead on, my potato-faced friend. Time's a-wasting!"

"Welcome to Fizzledump," Deeb Rauber said, grimacing as if he'd just bitten into an overly garlicked pickle. "You sure this place is worth saving? Seems like the monster could only improve things around here."

He and his reluctant guide were sloshing down Fizzledorf's muddy main road on horseback.

"It used to look a lot nicer," Bozworth said. He steered their mount while the Bandit King sat backward behind him, his feet resting up on the horse's hindquarters. "The monster has done a lot of damage."

"Monsters can't make a place boring, Bozworth. Seriously, check out that sorry excuse for a domicile over there," Deeb said as they passed a tiny thatch-roofed cottage. "Bland walls, bland doors. I'm half tempted to throw a rock through those dull little windows, but that would be a waste of rock. Whatever loser lives there isn't worth my vandalism."

The portly messenger pouted. "That's my house."

"Ha! Called that one!" Deeb crowed. "You get what I'm talking about, though, right, Boz? This town has no sense of style. These people aren't going to be ready for the likes of me." Before leaving his castle in Rauberia three days earlier, Deeb had changed into a blue velvet suit—stolen from the young prince of Valerium—and accessorized it with the long-lost crown of the emperor of Frostheim. He'd kept his finery clean during their travels mostly by having Bozworth carry him whenever they got off the horse.

Bozworth pulled back on the reins as drearily clothed villagers began to file out of their homes and fill the street. The messenger hopped down to exchange hugs and handshakes with his neighbors, but Deeb remained in his saddle, surveying the sea of gray linen and burlap before him. "Jeez," he muttered. "Has nobody in this town heard of *color*?"

A middle-aged woman in a nondescript gray dress peered up at him. "You look awful young for a Prince Charming," she said. "Which one are you supposed to be?"

"Charming? Ha!" Deeb stood up on his horse. "Listen up, Fizzledorks. You may have placed an order for the

League of Pimples, because you thought that was your only option, but you lucked out—you got me instead! Bozworth told me all about your little monster problem, and I'm going to take care of it."

Several villagers smacked the messenger with their plain gray hats, and one kicked him in the shin.

"Who are you?" one man asked Deeb.

Deeb threw his arms wide and thrust his chest forward. "I am . . . the Bandit King!"

A displeased murmuring rose from the crowd.

"You're just a kid," exclaimed one elderly woman, waving her boringly straight walking stick.

Deeb fought back the urge to spit on the entire populace of Fizzledorf. "Look, lady, I'm gonna let that slide because you're about a hundred and ninety, and even Bozworth probably looks like a schoolboy to you. But the rest of you better understand this: next person to use the K-word gets a bagful of fire ants poured down their shirt." With his toe, he nudged a squirming sack tied to the saddle, and the crowd's murmuring abruptly stopped.

"Yeah, I thought so," Deeb said smugly.

"You're really the Bandit King?" asked a woman in a gray bonnet. "Like from all those stories?"

"In the flesh."

"Are you going to rob us?" a man inquired.

"Possibly. I haven't decided. But either way, I *am* going to put an end to your monster."

"He really does want to solve our problem with the beast," said Bozworth, shielding his face with his hands for fear of getting hit again. "And I say we let him try. He may not be the hero we were hoping for, but—"

"Oh, I'm not a hero at all," Deeb said, using Bozworth's bald head as a step on his way down from the horse. "But heroes are overrated. They have to deal with so many unnecessary obstacles, like codes of honor, and ethics, and whether or not something is the 'right thing to do.' When you need a job done fast, call a villain. So, where's this monster of yours?"

The villagers all started talking at once, and Deeb whistled loudly to cut them off. "I need *one* person to assist me. One," he said. "And not Bozworth. I am *so* Bozworth-ed out. You, in the hood—I'm deputizing you."

Deeb pointed to a gum-chewing girl about his age. She'd joined the crowd a bit later than the others, but Deeb's eyes were drawn to her instantly; she was the only person in town wearing something that wasn't gray. "Sweet!" she said.

"Nice little red hood-and-cape combo you've got there,"

Deeb said. "Stands out."

"Thanks. My granny made it for me," the girl replied. "I wear it all the time. That's why everyone calls me 'Red.'"

The Bandit King nodded. "I'm gonna call you 'Hood.'"

The girl narrowed her eyes at him from under her dark cowl. "Then I'm gonna call *you* 'Woodsy,' 'cause you came out of the woods."

"I'm the Bandit King. Call me Bandit King."

"Yeah, good luck with that, Woodsy," the girl said with a smirk. "Anyways, nobody knows where the monster goes during the day. It shows up in town almost every day around dusk, chases people, wrecks stuff, and then runs off again."

"Hmm. That appears to leave us with two options," Deeb said. "We wait until dusk and attack the monster when it shows up or we find the thing's daytime lair and kill it while it sleeps."

"First one!" the girl shouted gleefully. "Attack the monster! Attack the monster!"

Deeb jumped back. "Whoa, there, Hoodsy. While I appreciate your enthusiasm for violence, I'm gonna tell you why I think option number two is the better choice."

"Because it's the safer one?" the girl asked flatly.

That *was* the reason, but Deeb wasn't about to admit

that. "Because it's the more devious and wicked way to do it," he said in a sinister tone. He squinted at the townsfolk. "Let it be known that the Bandit King is not above coming after you while you're asleep."

Hood nodded. "Nice."

"Any questions before we begin?" Deeb asked.

"Yeah," said the girl. "Who's Bozworth?"

The Bandit King was befuddled. "The pasty bald guy," Deeb said, pointing. "The one who brought me here."

Hood snickered. "That's Roger Thistlewit," she said.

"Thistlewit?" Deeb eyed the man, who nodded sheepishly. "Then why have I been calling you 'Bozworth'?"

"I've been wondering that for three days," he said. "But I was afraid to correct you."

Deeb shrugged. "That was a good call on your part. I probably would have poured the fire ants down your shirt. Come on, Hoodsy, let's go."

"Let's," Hood said with a smile. "Can I try on your crown?"

He tossed the jewel-encrusted headpiece to her. "Keep it," he said. "I've got twelve."

The girl pulled down her hood to reveal a head of lush black curls, upon which she placed the glittering crown. Her eyes seemed to glitter as well. And her teeth. And,

14

somehow, her earlobes. Deeb felt suddenly overheated in his velvet suit. He snatched the crown back off her head.

"You were better with the hood up," he blurted.

Hood led the Bandit King to various spots up and down the street, pointing out paw prints in bare dirt yards and claw marks on unpainted wooden doors. The rest of the Fizzledorfers followed in a tight clump, listening as the two would-be detectives discussed the clues.

"So, you ever seen this monster yourself?" Deeb asked as Hood ran around on all fours, growling, to demonstrate how the beast had ruined one family's grassless lawn.

"No," the girl said. "But my granny has. And she told me to run like the willikers if I ever even catch a glimpse of the thing. But Granny's old. She's sick all the time. She uses words like 'willikers.' Of course she'd say to run away. But running away's not really my thing."

"You don't seem like you fit in around here much," Deeb said. "How'd you end up—"

"Ooh! I know where to take you!" Hood bounced on her toes. "The pigs!"

"Yes!" Deeb said. "Take me to the three pigs. They survived a close encounter with this monster; they should be able to tell me something about it."

Hood grabbed Deeb by the hand—which sent his cheeks into a rapid flush—and half dragged him down to the end of the road, where there lay two large piles of debris and one simple, stonework house. Hood banged on the door.

"Who is it?" a small voice asked from inside.

"The Bandit King," Deeb said.

"Ack!" the voice screamed.

"He's with *me*," said Hood. "Open up."

"You're not much better, Red," said a second voice. Deeb raised an eyebrow at this. "Can't you please just go away? Haven't we suffered enough?"

"We're here to stop the monster," Hood said. "Open the door now, or I will drop another stink bomb down your chimney."

"Another?" Deeb asked with admiration as they heard several bolts slide back, and the door opened a crack. Hood pushed it open all the way, and they marched in.

The first thing Deeb noticed upon entering the home of the three pigs was the stench—it smelled worse than an ogre's outhouse. It was also covered with dirty clothes and food scraps that littered every surface. And there were no actual pigs.

"Aw, man," the Bandit King griped. "You're just people? Filthy, grime-covered people? There's no talking pigs here?" But his scowl quickly morphed into a grin. "Heh-heh. Actually, that's pretty funny."

"Thank you," said Hood. She leaned over and whispered into his ear, "The bards may have had a little help coming up with that idea."

Deeb snorted.

"It's a very insulting song," said the youngest of the "pigs," a man in greasy overalls, who had a huge dollop of dried oatmeal caked between his eyebrows.

"Way I see it, you guys coulda been called a lot worse," Deeb said. "Have you looked in a mirror lately?"

"We would," said the middle sibling, a tangle-haired sister with crusty nostrils. "But it's hard to see yourself through all the pancake batter spattered on there."

"Okay, we've established that you people are disgusting," Deeb said, grabbing a chair. "Now let's get down to business. I've got a monster to— Holy muttonshanks! What did I just sit in? Eh, I think I'm gonna stand. So, where were we? Oh, yeah. Tell me about the monster."

"Well, it had great big eyes," said the youngest sibling. "And great big ears. And a great big snout. And—"

"A wolf. It looked like a wolf," the sister said. "Wolves are about seven feet tall and walk on two legs, right?"

"How did you all manage to survive?" Deeb asked.

"That would be thanks to me," said the oldest sibling. "I'm Solly; I'm the smart one." He tapped his head to show everyone that he knew where his brain was, and several old peas fell out of his hair. "My brother, Rufus, went and got himself attacked first, and my sister, Petunia, got it second. But *I* was smart enough to get attacked third. By the time the wolf-monster got to me, the sun was coming up, and it ran away. I didn't have to do nothing. That's smart." He sat back and crossed his arms, a satisfied smile on his filthy face.

"So basically, you were saved by the sunrise," Hood said. The younger siblings nodded.

"Hey, this is my investigation," Deeb snipped. "I'll ask the questions."

"Sorry, Your Majesty," Hood drawled.

Deeb smiled proudly. "It's about time someone started addressing me by my proper title."

Hood slapped her forehead. "Aw, man. I forgot you were actually king of something. I was trying to be sarcastic."

Deeb shot her a dirty look before returning his attention to the eyewitnesses. "Which way did Old Big Bad go when he ran off?"

"Back that way, into the woods," said Petunia, pointing to the rear of the cottage. "But when it left, it wasn't very—"

Hood gasped. "Granny lives back there!"

"In the woods?" Deeb asked. "By herself?"

Hood nodded. "Believe me, she'd be even farther from this village if she could. She's always hated it here. It's so boring."

"Tell me about it," Deeb said. "These three slobs are the most interesting things in town. And just being in the same room with 'em makes me wanna barf."

"We can hear you, you know," said the younger brother.

"Look, if the beast's lair is anywhere near Granny's house, I've gotta go warn her," Hood said. "She's old and sickly. In fact, I was supposed to bring her a basket of muffins just this morning. But then that weaselly-eyed kid from the hill started looking at me, and I had to chuck the muffins at his big, dumb forehead. Well, I suppose I didn't *have* to, but I did, and now— What was I saying? Oh, yeah—Granny! Sorry, Woodsy, I gotta go."

"Wait," Deeb cried as she darted out the door. "What about our investigation?"

"There will be no more investigation!" shouted a red-faced man who plowed through the crowd of onlookers to block the Bandit King's path. The newcomer's ruffled collar and tall hat made him look like a circus clown compared to the other residents of Fizzledorf. "How many times have

I warned you all? How many times have I decreed that the monster is off-limits?"

"Thirty-seven," said the pig sister.

"Well, consider this your thirty-eighth and final warning," the man growled, his temples throbbing. "In the name of safety, no Fizzledorfer may attempt to hunt the monster, track the monster, or otherwise seek out any information about the monster."

"Gee, that's not weird or suspicious at all," Deeb snarked. "But whatever, High-Hat. *I'm* the one conducting this investigation, and I'm not a Fizzledoofus. For your information, I happen to be—"

"Where did this gaudily dressed moppet come from?" the angry man snapped, looking straight over the Bandit King's head. "One of you must have brought him here. Who?"

"Okay, first off, I have no idea what a moppet is," Deeb said. "But if it means 'kid,' I've got a bag of fire ants I need to crack open. And secondly, it was Bozworth."

"Who?" the man asked.

"He's here because of me, Vulpin," Hood said, stepping forward. "This town is never gonna be free of the monster if we keep waiting for you to handle it. So I sent for help."

The man gave her a steely-eyed stare. "You will address

me as *Mayor* Vulpin, young lady. Do not forget your place just because of our familial relationship."

"Our familial relationship doesn't exist," Hood shot back. "Not yet, anyway." She turned to Deeb. "The mayor here has been courting my granny. I don't know what she sees in him."

"So, you think just 'cause you run this dump, you can tell me what to do, eh?" Deeb said, shooting his own steely-eyed gaze back at Vulpin. "Well, I happen to be the one and only *Bandit King*. And while I may not be up on my social studies lessons—because school is for losers—I'm pretty sure a king outranks a mayor."

"The Bandit King? Oh, really?" Vulpin's lips curled downward in contempt. "While I don't believe for a second that you really are the notorious Deeb Rauber, I'll play along and pretend you are. In which case, there are approximately eight hundred outstanding warrants for your arrest. Constables, place the 'Bandit King' in one of our jail cells. And hurry, it's nearing sundown."

Deeb laughed. "Oh, right. Like you're going to— Hey, stop! What are you losers doing? Put me down!" But there was not much that one thirteen-year-old—even a notoriously wicked one—could do to prevent eight officers in drab gray uniforms from picking him up and hauling him down the road.

"And now for you, young lady," he heard Vulpin say. "Where are you? Red! Where did you go? Someone find that girl! No, never mind! Everybody into your homes! The sun has started to set. I'll take care of that brat myself."

As Deeb was carried into a dull, stone jail—and locked into a dull, stone cell—he found himself facing an unusual dilemma. He was pretty sure the girl in the hood was going to get him out of this predicament somehow. And he wasn't sure how he felt about that.

The next hour was excruciating for Deeb. He paced his small cell, waiting for a rescue he was sure to come—and which he planned to complain about thoroughly when it happened, insisting that he, the dreaded Bandit King, didn't need anybody's help, especially that of a snot-nosed girl in a hood who was too big for her own—

Crash! Bang! Thump!

"Ooh! She's here!" Deeb jammed his head between the bars and peered down the hall to where the guards had been stationed. He bit his lower lip in anticipation as he watched a head full of black curls appear from around the corner. But then he grimaced, because those curls had gooey strands of melted cheese tangled among them.

"You?" He spit the word from his mouth like a bite of moldy beef. "What are you doing here? Where's the Hood?"

"She sent me to break you out," said Petunia, the sister from the pig family, as she unlocked Deeb's cell with the key she'd just stolen from the guards.

"But why?"

"She said if I did this for her, she'd stop throwing stink bombs down our chimney."

"Heh. That probably just means she'll start throwing 'em in through the window instead." Deeb snickered. "But why didn't she come herself?"

"She had to get to her grandmother before the werewolf did," mumbled Petunia, who grew gloomy upon realizing that Deeb was probably right about the stink bombs.

"Wait—werewolf?"

"Um, yeah, that's what she figures the monster is," Petunia said. "I told her what I tried to tell you both earlier—that when the monster ran away from our house last month, I saw it get smaller and less hairy as it went. By the time it reached the end of the road, it was basically person-shaped. So Red thinks it's a werewolf."

"She's right!" In his excitement, Deeb grabbed Petunia's arm—but quickly let go for fear of contracting cooties. "And I know who the werewolf is, too. It's that grump-factory mayor of yours. That totally explains why he was all, 'Nobody look for the monster!' And why he was in such a rush to get out of there before sunset. 'Cause he was about to turn all fuzzy carnivore on us. And—Hoodsy's in trouble! The mayor will eat her the way he probably already ate her grandma. I've got to get to her!"

"Okay, good luck," Petunia said as Deeb dashed from the jail. Then she curled up for a nap inside his vacant cell, because it seemed like a much nicer place to stay than her brother's house.

Deeb Rauber ran as fast as his short legs could carry him, down the forest path that extended deep into the woods beyond the wrecked homes of the three pigs. He tripped a number of times, over rocks and roots invisible in the dark. His knees were scraped, his elegant suit scuffed, but none of it slowed him down. In fact, the only thing that did make him pause was the sudden realization that he was on his way to *help* someone. To *rescue* someone in trouble. To *save a life.*

Deeb hit the brakes.

What am I doing? he thought. *I'm the Bandit King, the most dreaded criminal in the Thirteen Kingdoms. I don't end troubles, I cause them. Why would I risk my own safety for some girl I barely know? When no one will even be around to see it?*

He stood among the moonlit trees and ran his fingers through his uncombed hair. *I should focus on staying alive until dawn and then take care of Mayor Monster Face when he's back in grouchy human form. That way I get the glory and none of the potential teeth marks.* He nodded to himself. *That's what I'm gonna do. That's what the Bandit King would—*

A scream interrupted his train of thought. The cottage was in sight, only a dozen yards away. And a clamor erupted from inside.

"Hoodsy."

Deeb ran to the house and threw open the door. The place was a wreck—overturned furniture, shattered plates, shredded linens—and Hood, backed into a corner by a ceiling-scraping, bristly furred, slobbering beast in a lavender nightgown.

Deeb quickly put it all together. Mayor Werewolf had gotten there first, devoured the grandmother, and then put on the world's worst disguise in order to trick Hood— which, apparently, had worked—and now the beast was about to wrap its enormous jaws around the poor girl's throat.

"Freeze, Kibble Breath!" Deeb shouted. "Yo you're big stuff, picking on old ladies and litt you're dealing with the Bandit King now. A you'll find that with the Bandit King, you can never quite expect—"

Clonk!

Hood clobbered the werewolf across the head with a broken bedpost. The creature collapsed.

"Thanks, Woodsy," Hood said. Her actual hood had fallen back, and Deeb could see her bright, glinting eyes as she smiled at him. "You showed up just when I needed you to."

It was one of the rare moments when Deeb Rauber had no idea how to respond. So he walked over to the unconscious werewolf and poked it with a stick.

"It's totally the mayor, you know," he said.

"Well, duh," Hood replied.

And as they watched, the body of the creature began to wriggle and writhe. It was changing back.

"I wasn't scared at all," Hood said. "Were you? I mean, I'd completely understand if you were; this guy turning into a man-eating wolf and all."

Deeb shrugged. "I used to know a guy who turned into a giant snake. This? Meh."

Within seconds, the furry, gray paws protruding from the nightgown became thin, bony, very human arms and legs. And the hideous, fanged face turned into that of a wrinkled old woman.

Deeb and Hood gaped at each other.

"Yeah, well, before, when I said, you know, about the mayor," Deeb stammered. "I was just, you know, testing you."

Two seconds later, Mayor Vulpin appeared in the doorway, panting. He saw Granny on the floor and ran to her side. "Oh, my dear, sweet Griselda!" He put his ear to her chest. "She's alive. But . . . you've seen, haven't you? You know."

Hood nodded. "My granny is the monster." All the energy and exuberance was gone from her voice. "How?"

"It was a curse—a horrible, evil curse," Vulpin said, cradling the head of his bride-to-be, "placed upon her by a spiteful fairy, simply because it hadn't gotten an invitation to our engagement party. Now do you understand, though? Why I had to do the things I did?" The mayor began to weep. "I just wanted to protect her. I love her."

"I understand," Hood said, her own eyes welling up. "But the rest of the villagers won't. If they find out, they'll hunt her down and slay her. Isn't there anything we can do?"

"Not unless you know some way to remove a magic curse," Vulpin said.

"Well, actually," Deeb said. He said it without stroking

an imaginary mustache. He said it without puffing out his chest or dusting off his velvet jacket. He said it without thinking at all. Because the words came from somewhere other than the Bandit King's diabolical brain. "Actually, I do."

Three months later, while Deeb Rauber sat upon his throne, dunking an unpaid-for scone into a mug of smuggled Maldinian cocoa, Vero took a break from practicing his swordsmanship on a life-size troll doll.

"So, this thing that happened in Fizzledorf, will you never tell me?" asked the bandit deputy.

"I did tell you, Vero," Deeb replied with his mouth full. "Nothing happened in Fizzledirt. There was no monster, no danger, nothing to outdo the princes on. It's a dead dump of a town. BORing."

"But am I not to think it peculiar that when you come home from Fizzledorf, you suddenly decide to free the leprechaun?" Vero asked, using the tip of his sword to pluck a creampuff from a silver platter.

"You looking to move into his cell?" Deeb replied.

"And that new bard song," Vero continued undaunted. "'The Tale of the Red Riding Hood,' it takes place in Fizzledorf, yes? Around the same time you were there?

You did not see this Bad Big Wolf? Or this nameless 'Woodsman' who helped save the day?"

"Ha! Woodsman. If the guy even exists, I'm sure he's just some lame do-gooder like those goobers in the League of Princes." Deeb leaned forward and narrowed his eyes at Vero. "Look, Fizzledorf is over. I want nothing to do with that rathole ever again."

Vero reached into his belt and pulled out a folded parchment. "Why, then, did the potato-faced man return here today with a wedding invitation? Which he says is for you, but which is made out to someone with the name of Woodsy? And which is signed by a Hoodsy?"

Deeb leaped forward and grabbed the paper from Vero. He crumpled it without looking at it and tossed it into a barrel full of used cupcake wrappers. "I am the Bandit King," he said, dusting off his suit and puffing out his chest. He paused to dramatically twirl a nonexistent mustache. "It's about time I reminded people of that. Go round up all my men. I'm about to plan the biggest heist the Thirteen Kingdoms has ever seen. I'll get those bards talking about me again if it's the last thing I do."

"Yes, sir," Vero said with a grin. "I may never find out what happened to you in this Fizzledorf place, but I believe it was a good thing you went, no? I believe that the old you is, as they say in my country, *back*."

"I hate your country," said Deeb.

Vero bowed and walked off to gather the rest of the bandit army.

And in the solitude of the vast, echoing treasure chamber—stuffed to its rafters with gold, jewels, and frosted pastries—the Bandit King's hand shot deep into a nearby barrel and began rooting through the trash.

FIRST CROSSING
BY PAM MUÑOZ RYAN

Papa pointed to a bench in front of a liquor store, and Marco gratefully dropped onto it.

He looked up and down the street in downtown Tijuana as it swarmed with American tourists. The neighborhood, grimy and flagged with graffiti, was infused with an undeniable sense of mystery and danger, as if something illegal was about to happen. Marco already felt guilty for what he and Papa planned, even though he hadn't yet stepped across *la Linea*. Sure, it was the border to the United States, but no one called it that. It was the Line between success and failure.

Shop owners stood in front of their stalls calling out, "I make you good deal! Come in! I make you good price!"

Children ran up to *la turistas*, determined to sell gum. "Come on, lady, you like gum? *Chiclets?* Everybody like gum." Vendors carried giant bouquets of paper flowers and hurried toward cars on the street, trying to make sales through open windows. It seemed that no one accepted no for an answer. The Mexicans simply begged until the tourists pulled out their wallets.

Marco added up the hours he had been on a bus from his home in Jocotepec, Jalisco, in order to reach Tijuana. Eighteen hours? Twenty-three hours? It was all a blur of sleeping and sitting in stations and huddling as close to his father as possible so he would not have to smell the sweat of strangers. Now they were finally in the border town, but their journey still was not over.

"Papa, I'm scared," he whispered.

"*No te apuras.* Do not worry," said Papa, reaching into a brown bag of peanuts. He calmly cracked one, peeled it, and let the shells drop onto the sidewalk.

Marco looked at him. Papa had the profile of an eagle: a brown bald head with a bird-of-prey profile. Once, when he was a little boy, Marco had seen a majestic carved wooden Indian in front of a cigar store in Guadalajara and had said, "Papa, that is you!" Papa had laughed but had to agree that the statue looked familiar. Marco looked just like Papa but with a mop of straight black hair. They had the same walnut-colored skin and hooked noses, but Papa's body was muscular and firm. Marco was skinny and angular, all knees and elbows.

"How do we find *el coyote*?" asked Marco.

"Do not worry," said Papa. "*El coyote* will find us. Like a real animal stalking its next meal, *el coyote* will sniff us out."

Marco took off his baseball cap, ran his fingers through his thick hair. He repositioned the hat and took a deep breath. "Papa, what happens if we get caught?"

"We hope it won't happen. But if it does"—Papa cracked a peanut—"we will have to spend a few hours at the border office. We stand in line. They ask us questions. We give them the names we discussed. They take our fingerprints. Then we make our way back here to Tijuana. *El coyote* will try to move us across again, tomorrow or the next day or even the next. It could take two attempts or a dozen. It is all part of the fee."

"How much?" asked Marco.

"Too much," said Papa. "It is how it is. Coyotes are a necessary evil."

"Are they bad?"

Papa sighed. "They are greedy. And money sometimes turns people into monsters."

35

Marco had heard stories about *coyotes*, the people who moved Mexicans across the border. Sometimes they took the money from poor peasants, disappeared, and left them stranded in Nogales or Tecate with no way home. *Coyotes* had been known to lead a group without enough water into the desert in the summer, where they were later found dead or almost dead, and riddled with cactus thorns. There were the stories about scorpion stings and rattlesnake bites after following a *coyote* into a dry riverbed. Just last week, Marco overheard a friend of Papa's tell about a group of people who hid in a truck under a camper shell, bodies piled upon bodies. The border patrol tried to stop the truck, but the *coyote* was drunk and tried to speed away. The truck overturned and seventeen Mexicans were killed. Since then, Marco's thoughts filled with his worst imaginings.

Papa saw the wrinkle in Marco's forehead and said, "I have always made it across. I would not keep doing this if it was not worth it. I would not do this if it was not the best thing for our family."

Marco nodded. It was the truth. Everything had been better for the family since Papa started crossing. He had not always worked in the United States. When Marco was younger, Papa had gone to work at a large construction site in Guadalajara, thirty miles away from their village of

Jocotepec. Six days a week, Papa had carried fifty-pound bags of rock and dirt from the bottom of a crater to the top of a hill. All day long, up and down the hill.

Marco had asked him once, "Do you count the times up and down the hill?"

"I do not count," he had answered. "I do not think. I just do it."

Papa's frustration had grown as the years went by. He was nothing more than *un burro*, a beast of burden. When the hole in the ground was dug and the big building finished, he had been sent to excavate another hole. And for what? A pitiful five dollars for his nine hours? The day that one of *los jefes*, the bosses, spat on his father, Papa set the fifty-pound bag down and began to walk away.

The boss laughed. "Where are you going? You need work? You better stay!"

Papa turned around and picked up the heavy bag. He stayed for the rest of the day so that he could collect his pay and get a ride home, but he never went back.

He told Mama, "My future and the future of my children are marked in stone here. Why not go to the other side? There, I will make fifty dollars a day, maybe more."

So it had been decided.

For the past three years, Marco and his family had seen

Papa only twice a year. He and his mother and younger sisters moved into a rhythm of existence without Papa. Marco woke with the roosters, went to school in the mornings, and helped Mama with Maria, Lilia, and Irma in the afternoon. During harvest he worked in the corn or chayote fields and counted the days until Papa would come home.

The money orders always preceded Papa. The income made Mama happy, and Papa became godlike in her eyes. They still did not own a house, but now they were able to pay the rent on time with plenty left over for things like a television and the clothes and games his sisters always wanted. They had money for the market and food, especially for the occasions when Papa came home and Mama cooked meat and sweets every day. The first few nights of his homecoming were always the same. Mama made birria, goat stew, and *capirotada*, bread pudding. Then Papa went out with his compadres to drink and to tell of his work in *los Estados*, the States. The family would have his company for a month, and then he would go back to that unknown place, disappearing on a bus, somewhere beyond the horizon.

"What is it like, Papa?" Marco always asked.

"I live in an apartment above a garage with eight messy men. We get up early, when it is still dark, to start our work in the flower fields. In the afternoon we go back to the apartment. We take turns going to the store to buy tortillas, a little meat, some fruit. There is a television, so we watch the Spanish stations. We talk about sports and Mexico and our families. There is room on the floor to sleep. On weekends we sometimes play *fútbol* at the school and drink a few cervezas. Sometimes we have regular work, but other times we go and stand on the corner in front of the lumberyard with the hope we will be picked up by the contractors who need someone to dig a ditch or some other job a gringo will not do. It goes on like this until it is time to come back to Mexico."

For several years Marco had begged to go with Papa. His parents finally decided now that he was twelve, he was old enough to help support the family. With both Marco and Papa working, his sisters might go to the Catholic school.

Mama had cried for three days before they left. When it was time to board the bus to Guadalajara, Marco hugged each of his sisters and finally, his mother. "Mama, I will be back."

"Some come back and some do not," she said, choking back her tears. "You and Papa . . . you are the family's *héroes*."

Marco knew he would return. He already looked

forward to *his* first homecoming, when he would be celebrated like Papa. As the bus pulled away from Jocotepec, Marco waved from the small window to the women in his family and, for the first time in his life, felt like a man.

Marco leaned back on the hard bench on the Tijuana street and closed his eyes. He already missed Jocotepec and his sisters playing in the cornfields behind the house. He even missed the annoying barking of the neighbor's dog and Mama's voice waking him too early for church on Sunday morning when he wanted to sleep.

Papa nudged him. "Stay close to me," he said, grabbing Marco's shirtsleeve.

Marco sat up and looked around. There was nothing unusual happening on the street. What had Papa seen?

A squat, full woman wrapped in a red shawl came down the sidewalk with a determined walk. Marco thought her shape resembled a small Volkswagen. Her blue-black hair was pulled back into a tight doughnut on the top of her head. Heavy makeup hid her face like a painted mask, and her red mouth was set in a straight line. As she passed she glanced at Papa and gave a quick nod.

"Let's go," he said.

"*That* is the coyote?" said Marco. "But it is a woman."

"Shhh," said Papa. "Follow me."

Marco wove between the tourists on the street, keeping Papa and the marching woman in his sight. She pulled out a cell phone and pressed it to her ear, talking into it as she turned off the main avenue and headed deeper into the town's neighborhood. Along the way others seemed to fall in with Papa and Marco until they were a group of eight, five men and three women. Up ahead, the *coyote* woman waited at a wooden gate built into the middle of a block of apartments. She opened it and signaled for the parade to follow her. They continued through a dirty *callejón* between two buildings, picking their way around garbage cans until they reached a door in the alley's wall.

"In there," she ordered.

Marco followed Papa inside. It seemed to be a small basement, with plaster walls and a cement floor. Narrow wooden stairs escalated one wall to someplace above. A lightbulb with a dangling chain hung in the middle of the room, and in the corner, a combination television and video player with stacks of children's videotapes was on the floor.

The woman shut the door. "Twelve hundred for each. American dollars."

Marco almost choked. He looked around at the others, who appeared to be peasants like him and Papa. Where would they get that kind of money? And how would Papa pay twenty-four hundred dollars for the two of them to cross the border?

The transients reached into their pockets for wallets, rolled up pant legs to get to small leather bags strapped around their legs, unzipped inside pouches of jackets, and were soon counting bills. Stacks of money appeared. The *coyote* walked to each person, wrote their names in a notebook, and collected the fees.

In his entire life Marco had never seen so much money in one room.

"*Escucha*. Listen. It is an election year, and *la Linea* is a big topic with the politicians. Border patrol is on alert. I have had trouble trying to get people across with false documents," she said, "so we will cross in the desert. I have vans and drivers to help. We will leave in the middle of the night. If you need to relieve yourself, there is a bathroom off the alley. You may leave one at a time to buy food at the corner market. The television does not work, only the video." Her cell phone beeped again. She put it to her ear and listened as she walked up the stairs that groaned and creaked under her weight. Marco heard a door close and a bolt latch.

*　*　*

It was almost dark. Marco and Papa found a spot on the concrete floor near the video player. Marco put his backpack behind him and leaned against it, protecting himself from the soiled wall, where hundreds of heads had rested.

One of the women, who was about Mama's age, smiled at Marco. The others, tired from their travels, settled on the floor and tried to maneuver their bags for support. No one said much.

A man next to Papa spoke quietly to him. His name was Javier, and he'd been crossing for twelve years. He had two lives, he said. One in the United States, and one in his village in Mexico. The first few years of work, he dreamed of the days he would go home to Mexico and his family, but now he admitted that he sometimes dreaded his trips back. He wanted to bring his wife and children with him to work and live in the United States, but they wouldn't come. Now he only went home once a year. What worried him was that he was starting to prefer his life in *los Estados* to his life in Mexico.

Papa nodded, as if he understood Javier.

Marco said nothing because he knew that Papa was just being polite. He would never prefer the United States to Mexico.

Marco was too nervous to sleep. He reached over and

took several videotapes from the pile. They were all animated movies. He put one in the machine, *The Lion King*, and turned the volume down low. Trancelike, he watched the lion Simba lose his father.

"Hakuna matata," sang the character on the video. "No worries."

A series of thoughts paraded through Marco's mind: the desert, snakes, the possibility of being separated from Papa, the *coyote*, scorpions. He closed his eyes, and the music in the video became the soundtrack of his nightmare.

Hours later, Papa woke Marco. "Now, *mijo*. Let us go."

Marco let Papa pull him up. He rubbed his eyes and tried to focus on the others who were heading out the door.

A man with a flashlight waited until they all gathered in a huddle. Flashlight Man wore all black, including his cap, the brim pulled down so far that all that could be seen were his black mustache and small narrow chin.

They picked their way through the alley again, following the direction of the man's light. On the street a paneled van waited, the motor running. The door slid open, and Marco could see that the seats had been removed to create a cavern. It was already filled with people, all standing up. Men and women held small suitcases and plastic garbage bags filled with their belongings next to them.

There didn't seem to be an inch of additional space until the Flashlight Man yelled, *"Mueva!"* Move!

The people in the van crammed closer together as each in the group of eight climbed inside.

"Más!" said Flashlight Man. The people tried to squash together. Papa jumped inside and grabbed Marco's hand, pulling him in, too, but Marco was still half out. The man shoved Marco like he was packing an already-stuffed suitcase. The others groaned and complained. The doors slid shut behind Marco. When the van surged forward, no one fell because there was no room to fall. Their bodies nested together, faces pressed against faces, like tightly bundled stalks of celery. Marco turned his head to avoid his neighbor's breath and found his nose pressed against another's ear.

The van headed east for a half hour. Then it stopped, the door slid open, and Flashlight Man directed them into the night. His cell phone rang to the tune of "Take Me Out to the Ball Game," and he quickly answered it.

"One hour. We will be there," he said into the phone. Then he turned to the small army of people and said, "Let your eyes adjust to the darkness. Then follow me."

Marco and Papa held back. They were the last in the

group forming the line of obedient lambs walking over a hill and down into a dry arroyo of rocks, dirt, and prickly grasses. Visions of snakes and lizards crowded Marco's mind. He was relieved when they climbed back up and continued to walk over the mostly barren ground. They crossed through a chain-link fence where an opening had been cut.

"Was that *la Linea*? Are we in the United States?" said Marco.

"Yes," said Papa. "Keep walking."

They walked along a dirt road for another half hour. In the distance, headlights blinked. Flashlight Man punched a number into his cell phone. The headlights came on again.

"That's it," said Flashlight Man, and they all hurried toward the van, where they were again sandwiched together inside.

That wasn't so bad, thought Marco as the van sped down another dirt road. A tiny bud of relief began to flower in his mind. *Hakuna matata*. No worries.

Within five minutes, the van slowed to a crawl and then stopped. Marco heard someone outside barking orders at the driver. The van door slid open, and four border patrol officers with guns drawn ordered them out.

Papa whispered to Marco, "Bad luck. *La migra*. Immigration officers. Say nothing."

They were herded into two waiting vans with long bench seats.

No one spoke on the ride to the border patrol station. What was there to say? They'd been caught. Inside, it was exactly as Papa had said. They stood in line, gave false names during a short interview, were fingerprinted, and then were released on the Mexico side of the border at the bus station.

"Now what?" asked Marco,

"We walk back to *la casa del coyote*," said Papa.

It was seven in the morning before they reached downtown Tijuana again. Most shops weren't open yet, and bars and fences enclosed the vendors' stalls that were filled with piñatas, leather goods, ceramics, and sombreros. Papa bought premade burritos and cans of Coke inside the corner market before they turned down the street that led to Coyote Lady's house.

Many of their group had already found their way back to the basement room off the alley. Papa and Marco found a spot against the wall and fell asleep. They woke late in the afternoon, Papa went again to the corner market for food. Marco watched the video *The Little Mermaid*, listening to the fish maiden's song, "Wanderin' free—wish I could be, part of that world."

It seemed everyone wanted to go to the other side.

Three days passed with the same routine: Papa going out for food, taking turns to use the bathroom off the alley, sitting and staring and waiting.

On Sunday morning Coyote Lady came down the stairs into the basement room. She wore a dress like the one Mama wore for church, a floral print with a white collar. Her face was scrubbed clean of makeup, and she looked like someone's aunt or a neighborhood woman from the village.

"Today is a big football game, professional, in San Diego. *La migra* will be eager to get people into the United States in time for the game. We start moving you in one hour, one at a time."

Marco looked at Papa. He did not want to be separated from him.

Papa asked, "How?"

"In a car," said Coyote Lady. "We hide you. If I only take one at a time across, the car does not ride low and look suspicious. I drive in a different lane each time across. As you can see, we are having trouble with the usual ways, so we try this. It has worked before, especially on a busy day."

Marco still didn't like the idea of being away from Papa. What happened if Papa got across and he didn't. Or what if he couldn't find Papa on the other side? Then what would he do? He didn't like this part of the journey. Suddenly, he wished he'd stayed home another year in Jocotepec. As if reading his mind, Papa said, "I will go before you, Marco," said Papa. "And I will wait for you. I will not leave until you arrive. And if you don't arrive, I will come back to this room. That will be the plan if we get separated."

Marco nodded.

Coyote Lady gave orders and signaled for one of the women to come with her. Every hour she stuck her head inside the room and called out another person.

Papa and Marco were the last of the group to go. They walked outside.

In the alley the trash cans had been pushed aside to make room for an old car. Flashlight Man waited beside the car, but he wasn't wearing his usual black uniform. Instead, he had on jeans, a blue-and-white football jersey, and a Chargers cap. He lifted the hood of the car.

Inside, a narrow rectangular coffee table had been placed next to the motor, forming a ledge. Two of the wooden legs disappeared into the bowels of the car, and two of the legs had been cut short and now provided the braces against the radiator and motor.

"Okay," he said. "You lie down in here. It only takes a

half hour. There is a van waiting for you in Chula Vista that will take you to your destinations."

Papa climbed up. Flashlight Man positioned his feet and legs so they would not touch the motor. Papa put his head and upper body on the tiny tabletop, curling his body to make it smaller. For an instant before the hood was closed, Papa's eyes caught Marco's, then looked away.

"*Vámanos,*" said Coyote Lady, and she wedged into the driver's seat. Flashlight Man sat on the passenger side. A Chargers football banner and blue pompoms sat on the dashboard as further proof of their deception. The car backed out of the alley and left.

Marco went back into the basement room and waited.

They had said it would take an hour, round trip. The minutes crawled by. Why did Papa agree to do this? Why did he humiliate himself in front of these people? Marco walked in circles.

After one hour he put in the videotape *Aladdin* and tried to pay attention as the characters sang about a whole new world. It seemed so easy in the video to get on a flying carpet to reach a magical place. *Where is my magic carpet? Where is the new world? Where is Papa? Did he get through?* Marco had never once heard a story of someone crossing while under the hood of a car. He tried to imagine being inside, next to the mechanics of the machinery. His stomach churned.

The door opened. Flashlight Man was back. "Let's go."

Marco took a deep breath and followed him.

The car was already positioned in the alley with the hood up. Coyote Lady took his backpack and threw it into the trunk. Marco climbed up on the bumper and swung his legs over the motor, then sat on the makeshift ledge. Flashlight Man arranged Marco's legs, as if he were in a running position, one leg up, knee bent. One leg straighter but slightly bent. Marco slowly lowered himself on his side and put his head on the tabletop. Then he crossed his arms around his chest and watched the sunlight disappear to a tiny crack as the hood was closed.

"Don't move in there," said Flashlight Man.

"I won't," he whispered.

The motor started. The noise hurt Marco's ears, and within minutes it was hot. The smell of motor oil and gasoline stung his nostrils. He breathed through his mouth, straining his lips toward the crack in the hood for fresh air. The car moved along for ten minutes until they reached the lanes of traffic that led to the border crossing. Then it was stop and go. Stop and go. His legs began to cramp, but Marco knew not to move one inch. He tried not to imagine what would happen if he rolled onto the car's motor.

The car lurched and stopped, over and over. Marco wanted to close his eyes, but he was afraid that he would feel disoriented. He watched the small crack between the car and hood, as if it were his lifeline. A flash of color obliterated his line of sunlight as a flower vendor stopped next to the car, trying to make one last sale to Coyote Lady and Flashlight Man. "*Flores, flores!* You buy cheap! You buy cheap!"

The car started to move forward, but the flower vendor continued to walk alongside, tapping on the window. Coyote Lady pressed on the horn. Marco's body trembled as the sound reverberated through his body. He inched his hands up to cover his ears. The vendor moved away, and the car began to move faster.

Marco never knew when they actually crossed the border. He only knew when the car began to speed up. His body pulsed with the vibrations of the car. Oddly, he watched beads of moisture move across the radiator, as if they had the ability to dance. Marco could not feel his right foot. It had fallen asleep. Panic crept into his chest and seized his muscles. He slowly pressed his hand back and forth across his chest to relieve the tightness. "No worries," he whispered. "*Hakuna matata.* No worries."

* * *

The car stopped, and a door slammed.

He heard someone fiddling with the hood latch. Light streamed into Marco's eyes, and he squinted. Flashlight Man pulled him from the car and handed over his backpack. Marco stumbled from his dead foot, and his body still rocked with the feeling of the moving car. He looked around. He was in a parking lot behind an auto shop.

Papa was waiting. "We made it," he said, smiling and clapping Marco on the back. "We are in Chula Vista, California."

Marco said nothing. He could barely hear what Papa had said because of the noise in his ears. Were they filled with cotton and bees? He felt as if his body had been insulted. He pulled away from Papa and climbed into a waiting van, this one with seats and windows. The door slid shut. Marco looked out the window and saw Coyote Lady and Flashlight Man driving away.

The others in the van smiled and talked, as if they'd all just come from a party. The relief of a successful crossing seemed to have unleashed their tongues. Marco listened as they talked of their jobs in towns he'd never heard of before: Escondido, Solana Beach, Poway, Cardiff. Papa told them that he and his son were going to Encinitas to work in the greenhouses and that it was his son's first time crossing over. Faces turned toward Marco.

Marco cringed, embarrassed, and stared at his shoes.

One of the men laughed out loud. "At least you were not rolled inside a mattress like I was on my first time!"

"Or like me," said a young woman, grinning. "They dressed me as an *abuelita*, a grandmother, with a wig and old clothes, and had me walk across with another woman's identification. I was shaking the entire time."

Marco looked up and forced a smile.

Stories spilled from their lips about their first times, or their friend's, or family member's: hiding inside hollowed-out bales of hay, cramped inside a hide-a-bed sofa in which the bed frame had been removed, buried in the middle of a truckload of crates filled with cackling chickens. Marco found himself laughing and nodding. He felt giddy as they reveled in one another's bizarre and sometimes life-threatening stories. And he began to feel proud and somehow connected to the people in the van. When one man told how he was hidden in a door panel of a truck, smashed in a fetal position for one hour and thought he might suffocate, Marco laughed the hardest.

"It is worth it, no?" said one man. "For our families. For a chance . . ." Tears filled his eyes.

As the people were dropped off in towns along the way north, they shook hands with Marco and Papa and left them with the same words, "*Buena suerte*," good luck. When Papa and Marco were the only ones left in the van, and the driver finally headed up Freeway 5 toward Encinitas, Papa grinned at him. "Okay?"

Marco nodded. "Okay." He looked out the window at the people in the cars on the freeway. And wondered how many of them were headed to a whole new world.

YIP
YIP
YIP

NEED THAT DOG
BY SHARON CREECH

The summer I turned twelve I decided that I needed a dog. It wasn't just that I *wanted* a dog; I *needed* it. It would make everything much better.

If I had a dog, I would always have a buddy at my side. He wouldn't go away for the summer like two of my friends had. If I had a dog, people like Valentino and his snarly sidekicks wouldn't bug me. They wouldn't look at me, walking along by myself, and think they could call me "a skinny squirt" and threaten to make me eat dirt.

I told my father about this urgent need for a dog.

"A dog, Sam?" my father said. "A dog?"

"You don't like the idea?"

"Oh, I like the idea just fine, Sam," my father said, but

the way he said it, in that sarcastic way, he meant exactly the opposite. "I like that idea about as much as you going outside and jumping into a mud puddle and coming back in and racing through the house and up over the furniture and knocking over a few plants on your way and then ferociously attacking those threatening pillows and then running back outside and rolling over a dead mouse and getting it all deep into your hair and then jumping back into the mud puddle and then digging up your mom's tulip bulbs and then coming back in and running another loop around the living room and—"

He did not like the idea.

My mother had a different reaction. She is a softie, through and through. She rescues spiders and worms and caterpillars. If a bird flies against a window and falls, stunned, to the ground, she stays with it until it recovers. She'll stop the car to help a turtle cross the road. She can't pass a dog or cat without pausing to say "Aw."

When I told her I needed a dog, she said, "Aw."

My dad heard that "Aw" and said, "No. No way."

My mom said, "But, aw—"

"No."

That didn't stop me from dreaming. I could see my dog clearly: a big German shepherd; black and tan; strong and sturdy; pointed ears alert to every sound; keen, watchful bright eyes. It was my loyal companion, my friend and my protector, walking proudly by my side. Valentino would not mess with me when I was walking my dog.

I brought home books from the library and left them strategically throughout the house: on the kitchen counter, the dining room table, the living room end table. These books included *Dogs for the Family* and *How to Train Your Puppy* and *Dogs Are the Best Pets* and *Every Kid Needs a Dog*.

Dad said, "Where are all these dog books coming from? Sam? Did you bring these home?"

Mom flipped one open and scanned the photos. "Aw."

"No," Dad said. "Don't even think about it."

"But, aw—"

The next day Mom came home from work all excited. "Sam! The perfect opportunity! Listen to this!"

I thought she was going to tell me that she'd heard about a free German shepherd puppy. Maybe someone at work was giving one away.

"Sam! A lady at work—"

I knew it!

"Has a dog—"

I knew it! "What kind of dog?"

"I don't know exactly, but a cute kind. And she wants—"

I was already picturing myself walking down the street with my new dog.

"Sam? Are you listening? She wants somebody to walk this dog while she's at work."

"What?"

"Are you even listening to me? She wants somebody to walk this dog while she's at work. Then feed it and play with it a little. I thought you'd be perfect! How about that? It's like having your own dog, only you don't have to pay for the food or the shots or the—"

"But—"

"Sam, listen. Maybe if your father saw you taking responsibility and being good with the dog, maybe he'd change his mind about having your own dog."

"But—"

"And she'd pay you, too!"

"What kind of dog is it?"

"I don't know. She says it's friendly."

"But is it a big dog or a little dog or a—"

"Sam, I don't know. You start tomorrow. Here's the address. She'll meet you there the first day—"

"Wait. You already told her I'd do it?"

"Yes, I did. Your dad will be so proud. You have a job!"

Dad did not seem all that impressed when Mom told

him about the dog-walking job.

"Doesn't sound very challenging," he said. "What if he loses the dog? What if he loses the key?"

So now I was worrying. What if I lose the dog? What if I lose the key?

The next day I met Mrs. Clicka and her dog. Mrs. Clicka was a tiny woman with curly brown hair. Her dog was a tiny, tiny dog with curly brown fur. Tiny, tiny, tiny dog, with a tiny name: Peep. I almost stepped on it. It went, "Yip, yip, yip, yip, yip, yip!"

This was not what I had in mind. "Are you sure it's a dog?" I asked. It looked more like a squirrel or a hedgehog.

"Of course I'm sure, you silly boy! Are you making a joke about little Peep?"

Mrs. Clicka gave me a three-page list of instructions and showed me where I would be able to find the house key. "Your mother says you're trustworthy. Yes?"

"Sure. That's me, Mr. Trustworthy." I stood up straight and tried to look trustworthy, but inside, my heart was saggy. I didn't like this tiny, tiny dog, and I was pretty sure it didn't like me, from the way it was curling its lip and baring its needle-teeth.

"Here's the leash. Now go on and take Peep around the block for a test run."

"Outside? You want me to take her outside? In public?"

"Are you making another joke? I don't understand kids these days. Of course, outside! Here's a poop bag. You do know how to scoop up poop, don't you?"

"Sure. Sure I do."

I did not know how to scoop poop, and I did not want to do it, and I was hoping I could pretend not to see Peep poop so I wouldn't have to scoop anything disgusting. To tell you the truth, I was more worried about being seen walking this little Peep dog, this little squirrely hedgehog-dog.

We started around the block. I was praying that we would not meet anyone who knew me, and I was in a hurry.

Peep was not in a hurry. She sniffed at every rock, at every tree, at every flower, at every ant, at every leaf.

"Come *on*," I urged. "Hurry up before someone sees me."

Peep did not like to be talked to that way. She raised her lip and showed me her needle-teeth. She squatted on my foot and peed on it before I realized what was happening.

"Oh, maaan, thanks a lot."

She took ahold of my shoelace and bit off a two-inch piece.

And then I heard it.

From across the street.

The voice of the dreaded Valentino.

"Heyyyy, Sammy boy, whatcha got there? What is it? A rat? A rabbit?"

Valentino was with two other guys. They joined in.

"Hey, is that your guard dog, kid?"

"Hey, you so fierce!"

They thought it was very funny, the sight of me and Peep. They laughed all the way down the street.

I was halfway back to Mrs. Clicka's house. If I could just make it a little—

"Heyyy, Sammy!"

I turned. It was Jenna and Jadeyn, twins in my class. I was surprised they even knew my name. They were tall and cool and smart, and I wanted to crawl in a hole. Now *they* were going to mock me, too?

"Heyyy, Sammy!" They were crossing the street, coming over to me.

They kneeled down in front of Peep.

"Awww," Jenna said. "Awwww, awwww, awww, isn't that the cutest little fluffball you ever saw?"

"Awww," Jadeyn said, "Awwww, awwww, awww, can I pet her?"

"Well, sure," I said. "Sure you can."

Then followed about a million "awwwwws" as they petted and giggled and kissed Peep.

Peep looked up at me as if to say, *See? Some people think I'm cute.*

"Can I walk her a little?" Jenna asked. "Can I hold the leash?"

"Well, sure."

And so we walked on, me and Jenna and Jadeyn and Peep. I am telling you, they *loved* that Peep.

And then Peep stopped and did her business.

I mean the *big* business.

And we three stood there trying not to watch.

And then I realized I had to pick up the business.

In front of the girls.

"Well!" Jenna said, handing the leash back to me. "We've gotta go!"

"Oh, yeah, bye-bye," Jadeyn said.

Once they were out of sight, I scooped the poop.

Disgusting. I don't know how people do this every day, walking their dogs up and down the street, watching them do their business right in front of everyone and then scooping up that business in a little plastic bag and then tying that little bag without touching the business and then walking on home, swinging that little bag that is obviously full of business, right there in front of the whole world.

Disgusting.

I decided to tell Mrs. Clicka that I was not able to take the job.

After Peep had sniffed every tree and hydrant and twig and leaf in a one-block area, we made it back to Mrs. Clicka's house.

She greeted us at the front door. "Oh! My little Peep baby. How was your walky? Was Sammy boy nice to you?" Mrs. Clicka unhooked the leash from Peep's collar and scooped her up in her arms and rubbed her face against Peep's. "Was he nice to you, mm, Peep baby, mm?"

"Mrs. Clicka," I said. "I don't think—"

Mrs. Clicka held Peep out to me, face-first. "Give-em Sammy boy a kiss for being such a big help."

She pushed Peep's face into mine. I saw a brief flicker of the needle-teeth and had a terrifying moment when I knew she was going to take a chunk out of my cheek.

"Kiss-em, Peep baby, kiss-em Sammy boy—"

And then there it was.

Dog slobber.

On my face.

A *lot* of dog slobber.

On my *face*.

"Ooh, looky there, Peep likes you! She *wuvs* you! You are definitely hired!"

"But—"

"Come tomorrow at three o'clock. The key will be under that rock—see?"

"But—"

"And I'll pay you at the end of the week."

On the way home, I thought, *Well, okay, I will do this for one week, and then she will pay me, and I won't have to do it anymore.*

That night I dreamed of dog slobber and dog poop and plastic bags flying through the air.

The next afternoon, trustworthy me managed to find the key to Mrs. Clicka's house, beneath the very obvious rock she had hidden it under. I say "very obvious" because on the top of the rock she'd drawn, in Magic Marker, a picture of a key. I mean really.

The key did not work. I tried this way. That way. Right side up. Upside down. I could hear Peep inside, her nails clicking on the tile floor as she ran in circles barking, "Arf, arf, arf, arf, arf, arfy, arf. Arf, arf, arf, arf, arf, arfy, arf."

Then I thought about my father. He often had trouble fixing things. His motto was *"If All Else Fails, Kick It."*

So I kicked the door. Tried the key. Turned the handle.

The door opened. Seriously.

And there was Peep, who took one look at me and backed up rapidly, her little legs racing, her paws slipping on the floor.

"Arf, arf arf, arf."

So much for the slobbery dog kisses of yesterday.

When I reached for the leash hanging on a hook near the door, Peep stopped arfing and cocked her head at me, this way and that. "Eep, eep, eep." I figured this meant she was excited; she wanted to go outside. Good.

We managed to walk the whole way around the block, with Peep sniffing at every little and large thing and peeing a dozen times and doing one big business—all without running into evil Valentino or his vile friends. No Jenna or Jadeyn either, though, which was a disappointment.

As we stopped in front of one last bush for Peep to inspect, someone called out. It was another girl in my class, Natasha, on a bicycle, coming down the street.

"Love that dog!" she said, coming to a stop beside me. I think those might have been the first three words she'd ever said to me. Natasha got off her bike and kneeled beside Peep, who rolled over onto her back, exposing her pale, pink stomach for Natasha to rub.

"Aw," Natasha said. "What a sweetness." Peep melted into blissful mush.

"This dog? 'Sweetness'?"

"Sweetness puddle love," Natasha cooed.

As I watched Natasha ride off, Peep peed on my shoe and bit off another piece of my shoelace.

And then I heard it.

From across the street.

The voice of the dreaded Valentino.

"Hey, Sammy boy, out walking your rat again? Why don'tcha put a little pink bow on it, Sammy boy?"

One of Valentino's vile friends chimed in. "Why don'tcha take it down to the garbage dump and let it find some dinner?"

Peep did not like that. "Arf, arf, arf, arf! Arf, arf, arf, arf!"

"Ooh," Valentino said, "you scare me, little rat dog, ooh!"

"Arf, arf, arf, arf, arf!"

Naturally, Peep took this opportunity to do another *big business* right there on the sidewalk.

"Ha, ha, ha!" Valentino and his vile friends laughed. "Ha, ha, ha!"

I stood there, staring at the little pile of big business, with Peep's leash in one hand and an already-used bag of business in the other.

"Pick it up, stick boy! Pick it up!"

The vile friends chanted, "Pick it up! Pick it up!"

I ignored the pile and pulled the arfing Peep up the drive and into Mrs. Clicka's house.

From a window I watched Valentino and his vile friends go on down the street.

I got another bag and went out and scooped the business.

Disgusting.

I did not want a dog, not if I had to do scoop duty every day. No thanks.

I filled Peep's water bowl and watched her slurp. She looked up at me. "Eep, eep, eep." Was she *smiling* at me? She rolled onto her back, paws in the air. "Eep, eep, eep."

"Okay, okay," I said. I rubbed her belly. She closed her eyes. I think she *smiled*.

The next day: got the key from under the key rock, put it into the lock, kicked the door, opened it, went in, and got Peep and the leash.

"Eep, eep, eep." Peep was hopping happy.

Off we went, in search of trees and bushes and sticks.

And then we heard it.

From across the street.

The voice of the dreaded Valentino.

"Heyyyy, Sammy boy—"

But at the same time, coming from the other way, were Jadeyn and Jenna and Natasha, strolling along hand-in-hand-in-hand that way girls do.

"Heyyy, Sammy!" they called. "Sammy!"

Valentino and his vile friends stopped.

Jadeyn and Jenna and Natasha surrounded Peep, embracing her with hugs and "aws."

"Aw, sweetness dog, aw, aw, aw."

"Sweetest, cutest dog *ever*."

"Aw, aw, aw—"

And then I heard it.

From across the street.

The dreaded *footsteps* of Valentino.

Coming toward us.

Followed by the vile friends.

Doomed.

Natasha said, "Aw, Sammy, you're so lucky."

"Me?"

Valentino and the vile friends were behind me.

"Oh, Sammy, if I had this cute little dog," Jadeyn said, "I'd never ever want to leave her ever, ever, ever."

Peep had been on her back, enjoying the belly rubs, but

when she saw Valentino, she rolled back over and stood there, legs rigid, neck stretched out, eyes big and round. She bared her needle-teeth.

"Rrrrrrr," she growled. "Rrrrrr."

I picked her up. I put her face up next to Valentino's.

Valentino blinked: once, twice, three times. His vile friends stood there like flagpoles.

And then Peep did it.

She licked his face. Dog slobber on the face of the vile Valentino.

He raised his hand.

He put it on top of Peep's head.

And he patted that head. And he said, "Aw."

Peep: My hero.

How I Became
Stink Daley
BY DEBORAH HOPKINSON

New York City
1858

My name is Danny Daley, but no one calls me "Danny"
anymore. These days, I'm known as "Stink." Before you
laugh, let me tell you how I got that nickname, because it's
not what you might think.

It began one Wednesday morning in March, not long
after I turned eleven. That was the day I met Daffodil—
and got my first whiff of the dairy stables.

I'd woken early on account of the thoughts swirling
in my head about what I had to do that day, and also
because my baby sister, Mary (better known as "Bitsy"),
just wouldn't stop crying. She gasped and heaved until her

little face turned red as a beet. (And in case you're wondering, I did *not* get my nickname because I've changed a lot of diapers. Yuck!)

"She kept your poor father awake most of the night," said Ma as she tried to feed a squirming Bitsy from one of those new modern baby bottles, with a hose for sucking out the milk.

"Oh, little miss Bitsy. You've got to be quiet, for Da's sake." I grabbed one of her tiny feet and tickled it. That used to make her gurgle and break into a toothless grin. Now Bitsy just pulled away from the bottle, rubbed her head against Ma's chest, and whimpered.

Bitsy had been a happy baby, but it seemed to me she cried a lot more lately. Or maybe it was just that, though she was only four months old, Bitsy somehow sensed that something bad had just happened to our family—and that all our lives were about to change.

On Monday, just two days earlier, my father had tumbled off a one-story building while on the job. It could have been a lot worse; as a bricklayer, he often worked on upper floors.

"No hospital," Da murmured as two men carried him up the narrow stairs to our third-floor tenement apartment.

74

He gritted his teeth to keep from crying out. Da reached out and clutched Ma's hand. "Promise me, Nora."

"Don't fret, Brendan. You'll not be leaving my sight," Ma assured him. Hospitals were feared in our neighborhood. Everyone on Prince Street had heard of someone who'd been taken off to one and never come home.

But Ma had insisted on sending for the doctor, who told us Da had a concussion, a strained back, and a broken right ankle. He'd need to stay home, maybe for weeks. The doctor didn't seem to care about Da not being able to work when he handed Ma his bill.

And neither would our landlord.

My older sister, Kathleen, stormed into action. She tore the last page out of my sketchbook and sat at the table scribbling numbers. When I was first learning to talk, I called her "Sis." The nickname stuck. (Though if you ask me, after Da's accident, "Bossy" suited her better.)

Later, when Sis showed Ma what she had done, our mother dabbed at her eyes. She didn't like to cry in front of us. She sighed. "There's no other way, is there?"

Sis shook her head.

"What?" I asked, looking from one serious face to the other. I reached out and grabbed the paper. Sis had added up the doctor's bill, along with the amounts we needed each week to pay the rent and to buy food and milk for the baby.

"Since Da's a bricklayer, he can earn a lot: a dollar and seventy-five cents a day. That's ten dollars and fifty cents a week," Sis told me. "The piecework sewing Ma does from home won't bring in enough."

That's when I understood. Women and children weren't paid much. It would take all three of us to earn what my father did.

"I'd hoped you could both stay in school until you were fifteen," Ma said. "Maybe you can go back someday. . . ." Her voice trailed off. But we didn't know how long it would take Da to recover, or if he'd ever get his old job back.

"It's fine, Ma," Sis said, putting her hand on Ma's. "I'm fourteen, after all. Tomorrow I'll find work as a seamstress. I should be able to earn five dollars a week, maybe six. I don't mind sewing in a shop."

That wasn't true, I knew. Sis would much rather be in school figuring arithmetic problems than counting stitches. She'd always talked about being a teacher. But if my sister was willing to give up her dreams to help the family, I knew what I had to do. I took a deep breath.

"I don't mind getting a job either," I said. "Maybe I can find work as an artist."

"An artist?" Sis rolled her eyes. She thought drawing was a waste of time. "You're a dreamer, Danny. No one *pays* artists."

"Yes, they do," I protested. "*Frank Leslie's Illustrated Newspaper* hires illustrators who go around the city and even sketch news events as they happen, and . . ."

I stopped. Of course, Sis was right. I might be a whiz with a pencil, but no one would hire me now—or maybe ever.

But what can I do to earn money? I wondered.

"Maybe I can milk cows," I said. "Grandpa taught me when I was little. He always said I had a knack for it. There are dairies here, aren't there?"

"I'm sure there are," Ma said, brightening. "Tomorrow morning I'll ask Mr. Timm, who delivers our milk."

"I won't let you down, Ma," I promised.

Later, when the room was dark, I pretended not to hear Sis crying on her thin mattress in the other corner. The next day, I went back to school—but only to say good-bye.

I'd made a promise and meant to keep it. But the moment I set foot in the stables on Wednesday morning, I wanted to race right out again.

"Have Danny go to Mr. Johnson's dairy. It's near his distillery on West Sixteenth Street and Ninth Avenue.

He should ask for Mr. Glander," Mr. Timm had told my mother.

I didn't have to worry about finding it. The distillery smelled bad enough, with its large chimneys spewing out plumes of black smoke. But all I had to do was to keep following my nose for another block. The smell of manure led me right to a large, muddy yard dotted with a few dilapidated sheds and several long narrow barns.

The stables weren't anything like the green pastures I'd imagined. Could this dairy be the home of the Pure Country Milk brand we fed Bitsy?

The doors of the largest barn stood open. When I stepped inside, I almost gagged from the stench. The air was thick and full of dust. Huge flies buzzed around my head. A filthy mix of mud and dung covered the wooden floorboards.

I put my hand over my nose and took a few more steps. Cows were packed into narrow stalls in two long rows. From the rear of each stall, manure seeped out in vile, black streams. There was a trough running along the front, so each cow could eat.

This is awful, I thought. *I can't work here.*

Just then, I heard a rustle at the open back of the nearest stall. A young calf stuck her head out from around her mother and stared at me with huge, curious eyes.

"Well, hello, little one," I said softly, walking toward her. She looked out of place, like a small flower poking its head up in the cracks of a sidewalk. My hand closed around the stub of a pencil in my pocket. It would be fun to try to capture her comical expression.

"Get away from that stall. What do you want here, boy?" A tall, bulky man appeared in the doorway and came striding toward me.

"I—I'm here to see Mr. Glander," I said, trying not to breathe in too deeply. The smell seemed to cling to my skin. The alley behind our tenement reeked, but it was nothing like this.

"I'm Glander. Who are you?"

I'd never been brave and bold like Sis, who would have stood tall and met the man's gaze without a second thought. But I tried.

"My name is Danny Daley. Mr. Timm delivers our milk," I began. "He said you lost your stableboy and might need another."

"Humph. You don't look strong enough to heft a shovel."

"I learned to milk cows when I was little, on my grandfather's farm back in Ireland," I said. "I can muck out stalls, too. I'm a hard worker."

"Is that so?" Mr. Glander narrowed his eyes and sized me up. He had thin, sandy hair and a long face, which put me in mind of Goldy, an old yellow horse Grandpa once had.

"All right. We'll try you out," he said. "You'll do the mucking out in the barns and shovel manure into the carts that haul it off. No milking. The milkmaids—we call 'em milkmaids, but they're all men—are the only ones allowed to feed and milk the cows.

"And stay out of the milk sheds. That's where we prepare the milk for delivery. You got that?"

"Yes, sir." I could already feel muck seeping through a hole on the bottom of my shoe.

"Be here at seven sharp tomorrow morning. I'll pay you fifty cents for a ten-hour day, six days a week."

My heart sank, but my sister had told me to expect this. "You have to ask for at least sixty cents a day, Danny. Otherwise, we won't have enough."

"I'm worth sixty-five cents a day, sir," I declared, surprising myself by my boldness.

Sis had made me practice. "Make sure you speak up, Danny. Look the man in the eye when you say your piece. It can't hurt to ask for more than what they first offer."

But now, seeing the stormy expression on Goldy Glander's

face, I wasn't so sure about that. "Cocky Irish lad, are you?" he asked. "Most boys would feel lucky to get fifty cents."

Most boys, I thought, *couldn't stand five minutes in a place like this.*

I waited, pressing my fingers into my palms. Sis had been quite firm on that point, too. "It's like haggling with a peddler on Mulberry Street. Once you offer your price, close your mouth. Let him speak next."

Mr. Glander glanced around. Then, maybe realizing I was the only boy to choose from, he said, "All right, sixty-five cents. But I'll dock your pay an hour for every minute you're late in the morning."

"Thank you, sir," I said. "I'll be on time." My sister might be bossy sometimes, but she had been right. This time I was glad I'd listened.

"All right, get outta here. I'll see you in the morning. And one more thing, Daley," Mr. Glander added. "I expect absolute loyalty from my workers."

"You have my word."

I didn't know then how much I would regret that answer. I scooted out of there as quickly as I could, not even caring if I stepped in a big pile of dung.

I did it! I thought as I got back out on the street. What I'd actually done (though I didn't know this yet, either) was to step right into the muck of one the greatest scandals to hit New York City.

"I got a job!" I almost sang the words as I wove in and out of the noisy crowds on my way home.

It felt good to be out in the sunshine. I took my time, gazing into the windows of Italian bakeries. The rows of crusty loaves of bread and trays of shiny fruit tarts made my mouth water. At a flower stall, I saw bright yellow daffodils, so fresh and sweet they made me think of the little calf.

Daffodil. I'll call her Daffodil, I thought. Not that she was mine, of course. But I was glad to know there would be at least one friendly creature to greet me the next morning. I had a feeling that the "milkmaids" might be as stern as their boss, Mr. Glander.

I also stopped to look at the latest issue of *Frank Leslie's Illustrated Newspaper*. Well, I couldn't *not* look at it! Each week there was a fantastic new illustration on the cover.

"I got my eye on you, boy," said the newsstand man as I reached for it. I stepped back and stuffed my fingers into my pockets. My right hand closed around the stub of my pencil.

Sixty-five cents. I'd be earning sixty-five cents a day. I

would turn it all over to Ma or Sis. I had a feeling Ma would be glad to let Sis keep watch on the family budget while she cared for Da and Bitsy.

Although I knew Sis would frown as she marked the cost on her tally sheet, I made up my mind right then to ask for six cents a week for myself, so I could buy the new issue of *Frank Leslie's Illustrated Newspaper* each Tuesday. I might even beg for a little extra for pencils and a note-book, too.

As far as needing new shoes, well, I wouldn't mention that right away. I'd just have to put up with the hole. The chance to pore over each issue of Frank Leslie's paper would be well worth a muddy wet foot.

During my first week as a stableboy, I learned three impor-tant things.

The first was to keep my head down and my mouth shut. If I didn't, one of the milkmaids who fed and milked the cows would box my ears and yell, "Get back to work, lazy Irish boy!"

Second, I found out that no matter how hard I worked to clean all the stalls (several barns with long rows of them), my task was hopeless: the stink just wouldn't go away.

And then there was the third thing: there was a reason

why the dairy smelled so bad. It wasn't only the cow dung. No, the stables reeked because of what the cows ate, which wasn't hay or grass or anything you might expect. I discovered this one day as I watched one of the milkmaids, a bulky man with a thick beard and filthy hands, pour foaming, hot liquid into a trough.

"What's that?"

"Swill, of course." Seeing my confused expression, he added, "It's waste from the distillery—a sort of grain mush left over from making the liquor. That's what we feed them."

"It's boiling hot!" I exclaimed, watching a cow step back as steam from the disgusting mush rose up in her face. "She can't eat it."

"It'll cool. They soon come to like it," the man assured me. "Works out well for Mr. Johnson, the owner. The swill is free waste, and we just cart it over from the distillery next door. We dump the rest in the river."

"I don't think swill can be good for the cows," I blurted. "I mean, some of them have sores on their backs and bad teeth. And their tails . . . their tails seem to be rotting off. A few have normal long tails, but others just have stubs left."

"Irish boy, let me tell you something about working here," he hissed, leaning so close I could smell his foul breath. "You just do your job, keep your head down . . ."

"And my mouth shut," I finished. "Sorry, I forgot."

"Don't forget again."

"Keep my head down. Keep my mouth shut." I repeated those words to myself many times in the weeks to come. My family needed me to keep this job. We needed the sixty-five cents I made each day.

But it got harder and harder to see Daffodil and the other cows in such misery. The manure I shoveled didn't look like normal cow dung. Instead, it was a sticky liquid, as if the cows had diarrhea.

And they had no room to move! Each cow was tied in a stall only about three feet wide. She could only stand up or lie down, but was never taken out into the fresh air or allowed to walk around.

Most of all, I could never get used to seeing those rotting tails.

After hearing about how awful the stables smelled, you might expect that was how I came to be called Stink. But that's not the reason either, although I admit I now reeked like an open sewer.

Remember how I'd worried about getting mud inside my shoe because of one hole? Well, every day that awful stuff covered the tops of my shoes, turned my pants black, and stained the sleeves of my shirt.

I'd be fibbing if I told you I didn't cry sometimes. Tears ran down my dirty cheeks, but I didn't dare wipe them off, or I'd get stinky gunk in my eyes and mouth. I just kept my head down and hoped none of the milkmaids noticed me.

I couldn't go home smelling that way. Our apartment was tiny—only two rooms and no bathtub. There weren't even any public baths in our neighborhood.

At least I did manage to find a solution to *that* problem. The stables weren't far from the Hudson River. Every day after work, I walked there to rinse off (upriver from where the distillery dumped the rest of its waste). Usually, my clothes had just enough time to dry on my thirty-minute walk home.

Sis still wrinkled her nose at me every night. I could never totally get rid of the smell that clung to my skin and hair. Mostly, though, I was able to fool my parents, who imagined me working on a small farm, hidden away in the midst of buildings on the outskirts of Manhattan.

As Mr. Glander had reminded me, most boys would be happy earning fifty cents a day. So I couldn't tell my family the whole truth—not about what I saw every day or how I wanted to quit that job more than anything.

How could I add to the problems we already had?

"I'm proud of you, Danny," Da had said when I'd told him how I'd asked for a higher wage. He was still lying flat, to help the pain in his back, with his right ankle propped up on a pillow. "Your grandpa would've been pleased, too. He always said you had the makings of a farmer."

We were silent, thinking of all we had lost in the potato famine. The disaster had struck all of Ireland, destroying crops and causing widespread starvation that killed many, including my four grandparents, and my baby brother, too. It was why we had left.

Bitsy, the only one of us born in America, had been named after Da's mother, Mary. "She is a gift and carries all our hopes for a new life," Ma had said when Bitsy was born.

No, until Da was well again, I'd have to do my part and stick it out. Besides, what could I do to change anything there?

Even so, I couldn't shake the feeling that by not saying anything, I was part of the bad things happening at the stables. Every day that I went to work, I felt more and more like the cows. But instead of sores on the outside, I had something rotten eating me up on the inside.

* * *

Over the next weeks my father got better slowly. But Bitsy seemed to grow worse. She cried constantly, her little legs kicking hard. Sometimes she rubbed her tummy like it hurt. And while she had been sleeping through the night, now she woke up several times, crying to be fed like a newborn. It was almost as if the milk didn't satisfy her. Once, when I saw Ma change her diaper, I was put in mind of the cows.

"Let her sleep out here with Danny and me from now on," Sis finally said, to give Ma a rest from getting up so much with the baby at night. "I'll give her a bottle when she stirs."

Helping Ma take care of Bitsy was Sis's responsibility, not mine. But the next night my sister was so worn out from bending over a sewing machine during the day that she didn't stir when Bitsy began to whimper beside her.

What else could I do? I got up and padded across the room. "Come on, Bitsy girl," I whispered, reaching down for her. "I'll give you a bottle."

We had a small icebox, where my mother kept the milk Mr. Timm delivered, and a few other things. I lit a lamp, and bouncing Bitsy on my shoulder, poured out milk from the larger container into her glass feeding bottle with its new, modern India rubber tube.

For the first time, I looked at it closely. If our Pure Country Milk came from the cows I saw every day, how pure could it be? Could what ailed Bitsy be caused by the milk?

There were milk sheds next to the barns, but I'd never been inside. That very first day, Mr. Glander had warned me to stay away from them. And he'd reminded me every week since. "Remember, boy, you got no business in the sheds," he'd say. "We use them to store milk before it's bottled and loaded onto carts."

Now I wondered what really went on inside those sheds. If someone caught me poking around them, I might lose my job. But as I looked down at my little sister's dark eyes in the lamplight, I decided that was a risk I had to take.

The next morning, I left home earlier than usual and ran the two miles to West 16th Street. I had my new pencil and a small notebook tucked into my back pocket. If anyone asked, I'd just say I wanted to sketch Daffodil.

I worked in several barns but always saved Daffodil's for last. That way, the men would be done feeding and milking, and I'd have the place to myself. I'd gotten into the habit of letting Daffodil loose. She loved to follow me around, sniffing at my heels. I wished I could take her with me to the river so she could feel the sun on her back, and even eat some real grass on the riverbank. I'd noticed Daffodil had already started to get ulcers like the other cows.

When I got to the dairy, I made my way across the mud and stood behind one of the milk sheds. The yard seemed deserted at first. I was about to dart inside when I spotted Mr. Glander and a man I didn't recognize coming out of a barn.

I ducked around the back of the shed just in time. I held my breath as they opened the door and went inside. There were cracks in the walls, and I found one large enough to peer through.

The light was dim, but I could just make out Mr. Glander standing over a large vat. The other man began pouring something into it while Mr. Glander stirred the mixture with a large wooden paddle.

"That's it. So, we water it down first, like this," Goldy Glander was saying. "Then we'll add that chalk, flour, and starch over there to thicken it again."

"What about the molasses?" the man asked. I guessed he was a new worker learning his job. But what exactly *was* that job? What were they doing to the milk?

"That comes last. Mr. Johnson likes us to use molasses

to give the milk a good color," Mr. Glander said with a low chuckle. "And that's how just one gallon of milk from the cows becomes several gallons of Pure Country Milk! Now it's ready to pour into cans and load onto the carts for delivery."

Delivery! So this is what we've been feeding Bitsy.

Before the men emerged, I slipped away quietly and made my way to the nearest barn. Grabbing a shovel, I got to work as usual. Inside, though, I was shaking.

For now I knew: Not only were the cows sick from being fed swill, Mr. Glander (following Mr. Johnson's orders) was watering down the swill milk. That way, the dairy could get as much money as possible. Even worse, the milk was being doctored with other substances—like chalk—to make up for the poor consistency and give it the appearance of farm-fresh milk.

Pure Country Milk was a lie. It was swill milk from cows with rotting teeth and tails. Babies shouldn't be drinking chalk and flour! It was making my baby sister sick.

I wondered if all the men who worked here knew what was added to the milk. They certainly knew about the condition of the cows—and that some cows that died were even sold as meat.

But maybe the men didn't care. They just kept their

heads down and their mouths shut. And they did their jobs.

Like me, I realized. *I'm as bad as them.* For weeks I'd known about the sick cows with rotting tails. But I'd been too scared of losing my job to tell anyone.

I had to make sure Ma stopped feeding Bitsy swill milk. I knew we bought this kind because it was supposed to be good—but also because it was cheap.

But my little sister couldn't be the only baby getting sick. What about babies and children from other poor families who were drinking it, too?

By the time Mr. Glander came into the barn at seven to check on me, I was busy mucking out a stall as usual.

"Good morning, Mr. Glander," I said cheerily. My hands were still shaking, and my head was still whirling with confused thoughts, but I couldn't let him see that.

"Get over to the big barn, Daley," he ordered. "Mullen needs your help."

"Right away, sir," I replied.

Mr. Mullen was waiting for me near Daffodil's stall.

"We got a dead one to sell as meat. Help me haul 'er outta here," he said shortly. "You should be strong enough for that. The mother's upset."

He moved to the side. That's when I saw Daffodil lying stiff on the ground beside her mother.

I stared, unable to move. My heart pounded, and I pressed my nails into my palms to keep from crying.

"Well, come on. I got other work," he barked. "Grab her hind legs. We'll load her onto a cart to be hauled off."

That's when I made up my mind.

I'd never drawn Daffodil while she was alive. But I'd do it now.

Somehow I got through the rest of the day. On my way home I bought the new issue of *Frank Leslie's Illustrated Newspaper* with the six cents I had in my pocket.

I stood pressed against a building, away from the crowds rushing past me. I searched until I found what I was looking for, and then I made my plan.

"What are you drawing?" Sis asked later that evening, trying to peek over my shoulder. She was pacing the floor, bouncing Bitsy on her hip to get her to sleep. "You've been making sketches all night."

"Nothing much," I said, covering my paper with one hand. "Just drawing baseball players." She would believe that, I figured.

Every boy on Prince Street, me included, was excited

about the New York Knickerbockers and the new association of baseball clubs formed just last year. If I hadn't been working such long hours, I'd be out in the alley playing.

But my sister wasn't fooled that easily.

"I can always tell when you're lying, Danny," she whispered. She glanced toward the other room, where our parents lay asleep. She patted Bitsy's soft hair. "I know something's wrong. You can trust me—I'm your sister."

At first I hesitated. But I had to tell someone.

"I . . . I haven't wanted to say anything, because we need the money I earn at the dairy. But, Sis, that dairy is a bad place. We have to stop feeding Bitsy milk from there. It's making her sick. I just know it."

"What do you mean, Danny?"

I opened the notebook and pointed at a sketch. "This shows how crowded the stalls are."

Turning the page, I said, "The cows get sick from eating the swill from the distillery. This is what happens to their tails. This is a picture of a calf that died today."

Sis gasped. Then I showed her my last drawing. "And this shows men adding flour and chalk to the milk we buy for Bitsy."

My sister sank into the chair beside me. Tears filled her

eyes, and she clasped Bitsy close. "Is this true, Danny?"

"Yes. And lots of poor families like us buy Pure Country Milk," I said softly. "Everyone believes they're feeding their babies good, fresh milk. But they're not."

Sis was quiet for a long moment. At last she said, "I'll talk to Ma about the milk. She can tell our neighbors, at least. But you can't go back there, Danny."

"I have to! We still need the money until Da is better." I gathered my drawings. "Besides, I . . . I need to find out more."

"What do you mean?"

"I want to make more drawings—to gather evidence."

She frowned. "It could be dangerous if they catch you."

"They won't catch me," I said.

Over the next two weeks, I was the perfect stableboy. I got to work early and stayed late. I kept my head down. I kept my mouth shut, and I didn't ask any questions.

But secretly, I kept my eyes open. And, just like Sis, I did a lot of arithmetic.

I counted the cows packed into each crowded barn and kept a tally of how many died each week. I counted the number of cows with only stubs for tails and how many had ulcers on their backs. I also counted those who had to be propped up in a sling to be milked because they were too sick to stand.

At night, I bent over my notebook, making sketches and writing down everything I'd learned. Da, who was hobbling about now, looked at me curiously.

"Is that arithmetic you're doing, Danny?" he asked one night. "I thought Kathleen was the one who liked figures."

"I'm giving Danny some problems to do so he can keep up," Sis put in quickly.

"Your mother and I are lucky," Da said. "This accident knocked the wind out of me. But I hope to send you both back to school by fall."

Then, just when I had all the information I needed, I got caught. It happened one afternoon when I went outside to get a drink of water at the pump. As I leaned over, my notebook fell out of my back pocket.

At first, I didn't realize Mr. Glander was standing behind me. But he was.

Not only that, but my notebook had landed open, showing a drawing of a cow in a sling. I looked down at it in horror. I wasn't fast enough. His boot landed on my outstretched fingers.

"What's this?"

"Give it back!" I cried, desperate.

He pushed me aside, picked up the notebook, and began turning the pages. His long face turned red with rage. "Why, you little scoundrel!"

I couldn't let him keep it. Without thinking, I lunged, kicking him hard in the shins and snatching the notebook from his hands. He reached for me, but I ducked and began running, slipping and squelching through puddles and mud and filth.

"Stop that boy!" Mr. Glander yelled.

But no one could. No one would.

I fell once, but I scrambled up and kept running. I ran out of the yard, past the distillery, and down Hudson Street. I ran all the way to the address I had memorized: 19 City Hall Square.

When I got there, I flung open the door. The sign on it read: FRANK LESLIE'S ILLUSTRATED NEWSPAPER.

"Hallo, there! Are you all right, lad?" A man got up from a desk. He looked startled to see me. No wonder: I was covered in mud and panting hard.

"Can we help you?" he asked.

I tried to catch my breath. My knees were weak.

"My name is Danny Daley," I gasped. I held out my

notebook. "I need to give this to Frank Leslie."

The man took it. "What's this all about, lad?"

"Swill milk." I panted. "Swill milk is hurting babies."

He turned over one page, then another. Once, he gave a low whistle. "This is true, what you've drawn here—about the cows and what they put into the milk?"

"Yes, sir. I work at the Sixteenth Street Dairy. My boss caught me with this. I grabbed it and ran."

"Ah. Well, you don't work there anymore," he said with a grin. "After this you can never go back."

He was right, of course. I had lost my job.

"How did you know to come here?" the man asked.

"I read the paper all the time. I looked up the address. I thought . . . I wanted . . ."

"You thought *Frank Leslie's Illustrated Newspaper* should take on the villains behind this scandal, is that it?"

Had I been wrong in coming here?

I thought of Bitsy. I raised my head and met his eyes. "Yes, sir. I do think so. Someone needs to expose this scandal. Babies are getting sick from this milk. Some might even have died. And the animals suffer, too."

It was the longest speech I'd ever made.

The man looked at me for a moment. Then he nodded and called out to a teenage boy nearby. "Thomas, can you bring a glass of water for our young hero here?"

"I'm not a hero at all! I was scared," I whispered, shaking my head. "I'm . . . I'm just an ordinary boy."

If I hadn't waited so long to act, I might have saved Daffodil. And maybe Bitsy wouldn't have gotten so sick.

"Most heroes are just ordinary people. And I'd bet most of them also feel scared at some point," the man said. "Now, come sit down. You look as if you're about to topple over."

"I shouldn't. I stink. And I'm covered in mud."

"Nonsense," said the man with a laugh. "Reporters are always up to their necks in mud, one way or the other. That's the only way to get the story."

I nodded, but I wasn't sure I believed him. "Is Mr. Leslie here today?"

"My boy, *I'm* Frank Leslie. Ah, here's your water." He took the glass from the boy and handed it to me. I gulped it down.

"And this is my crack illustrator, Thomas Nast, who's not much older than you. He's seventeen. Thomas, this is a boy who wants to make a stink about swill milk. His name is Danny Daley. Or better yet, I think we should call him 'Stink Daley.' Does that suit you, lad?"

Stink Daley. I grinned. "Yes, sir. I think it does."

Frank Leslie grinned too and reached out to shake my hand. "Welcome, Stink. You've come to the right place."

So, that's the story of how I got my name—and my start as an illustrator.

I learned three important things my first week as a part-time newsboy and apprentice artist at *Frank Leslie's Illustrated Newspaper*.

The first was to keep my head up.

The second was to raise my voice and never be afraid to make a stink.

And the third was always to ask hard questions, because that was the only way to get to the truth.

Mr. Leslie assigned me to work under Thomas Nast, who seemed glad not to be the youngest artist anymore. I worked ten hours a day to make my sketches perfect. But I had more fun doing it than anything I'd ever done.

And it turned out that the scandal was even bigger than I imagined. The Sixteenth Street Dairy wasn't the only one making swill milk. Mr. Leslie himself took on the investigation, visiting other dairies in New York City and Brooklyn, and discovered mistreated cows and contaminated milk. And Thomas drew more pictures for the story.

A few weeks later, in May of 1858, the front page of *Frank Leslie's Illustrated Newspaper* carried a startling exposure of the swill-milk trade, calling particular attention to the awful conditions at the Sixteenth Street Dairy owned by Mr. Johnson.

Mr. Leslie paid a call on my parents to give them a copy of the paper and tell them how proud they should be of me. As you might expect, after meeting Kathleen, he was so impressed he offered my sister a part-time job in the paper's accounting department—on the condition that both of us go back to school.

I wish I could tell you our efforts led to the immediate downfall of distillery owners like Mr. Johnson and his friends, who tried to cover up the swill-milk scandal because profits were more important to them than people's health.

But those villains fought back tooth and nail.

In the end, it took years to pass laws to protect babies like Bitsy and many others who got sick or even died because of swill milk. It took the hard work of investigators like Frank Leslie and Thomas Nast.

And it took ordinary people brave enough to raise their voices and make a stink. Like Frank Leslie said, most heroes are just ordinary people.

People like me: Stink Daley.

AUTHOR'S NOTE

"How I Became Stink Daley" is historical fiction based on real events. While Danny and his family are imagined, there really was a swill-milk scandal in the mid-1800s in New York City.

Thanks to the investigative journalists and artists of *Frank Leslie's Illustrated Newspaper*, the scandal was exposed in its May 8, 1858, issue with the lead article entitled "Startling Exposure of the Milk Trade of New York and Brooklyn." Among the Leslie artists was the eighteen-year-old Thomas Nast, a political cartoonist who later became known as "Father of the American cartoon."

The issue drew attention to distilleries that ran dairies that fed cows the swill, or waste, from the distillery process. The animals were packed into crowded barns in stalls three feet by eleven feet. Many suffered from diseases such as distemper. The swill milk, suspected as a cause of infant death, was doctored by adding other substances to stretch the quantities, including water, flour, molasses, chalk, and plaster of Paris.

Responding to public outrage, the board of health established a committee to review the allegations. It was headed by a politician named Michael "Butcher Mike" Tuomey, who had—with several other members—conspired in a cover-up by secretly warning distillery owners as to when inspections were going to take place, so that diseased cows could be removed and replaced with healthy ones. But reporters from Leslie's paper kept the committee members under watch and exposed Tuomey.

Even so, unsanitary and scandalous practices continued until the 1870s, and it wasn't until 1893—when a philanthropist named Nathan Straus helped to finance milk depots that sold clean, pasteurized milk to poor families in New York—that infant mortality rates dropped.

Corruption and cover-ups in milk and water and food are not simply the stuff of the past. In 2008 there was a scandal involving baby formula in China. In 2015 it was discovered that officials knew of high levels of lead in the water of Flint, Michigan, and did nothing until ordinary people became heroes and took action.

BIBLIOGRAPHY

Frank Leslie's Illustrated Newspaper. "Startling Exposure of the Milk Trade of New York and Brooklyn." May 8, 1858.

———. "The Swill Milk Committee Render Their Report at Last." July 10, 1858.

The New York Times. "They Ought to Be Beaten: 'Swill-Milk' Tuomey." October 29, 1878.

Wilson, Bee. *Swindled: The Dark History of Food Fraud, from Poisoned Candy to Counterfeit Coffee.* Princeton, NJ: Princeton University Press, 2008.

written by **Cathy Camper**   dibujos por **Raúl the Third**

108

112

114

118

120

122

126

KALASH

BY EUGENE YELCHIN

Ever since my brother and I nearly got ourselves killed speeding across Moscow, our relationship has taken a turn for the better. Up until that lunatic chase (tires gripping, brakes screeching, guns blaring), my brother and I had no relationship to speak of. For example, the day my brother walked into our flat after a two-year stint in the army, he didn't even say hello to me. Instead, he said hello to the TV and the couch. I might have even allowed my brother to waste his life away on our legless couch smelling of armpits if not for certain jackasses at school. For the two years that he had been away, my "bighearted" schoolmates had enjoyed knocking the living daylights out of me at recess. I'd taken to hiding in the boiler room of our school. If

I couldn't get my big brother off the couch and covering my back, the jackasses would bury me in snow and you wouldn't find my body until the spring melt.

"We are witnessing the coldest January on record," a cute lady said on TV, and opened her eyes real big. "A snowfall such as our Russian capital hasn't seen in one hundred and thirty years."

"Is that a fact?" I said. "That's stupid, lady. How can Moscow see anything? It's not a human person."

I laughed madly, hoping my brother would join me (he didn't). He hogged the couch, lolling on his belly, his skinny arm drooping down to the floor. The rolled-up shirtsleeve of his filthy thermal showed off a tattooed assault rifle, like the one he'd carried in the army, an AK-47.

"'Shed Blood for Mother Russia,'" I read aloud the words inked into his bluish skin below the gun. "Can I see your wounds?"

He grunted and turned onto his back, never taking his eyes off the cute lady on TV, but I wondered what he saw. He was nearly blind, always squinting through eyeglasses (thick as my finger, left lens cracked in half).

"What about medals? Can I see medals?"

The barrel of the AK-47 on his arm twitched a little as he scratched the seat of his army-issued long johns.

"If *I* had medals," I said, "I'd pin them on my chest and walk my little brother to school so his friends could see I shed blood for Mother Russia."

He squinted at me with disgust. "I'm not allowed to wear them."

The sound of his voice startled me; the first words he'd said to me since his return.

"You're not?" I said.

He slapped the couch lazily, looking for the TV remote, but couldn't find it. He was lying on it.

"I'm not allowed to wear my medals," he said, "because I was decorated for secret missions. I've been sent deep undercover behind enemy lines."

Everyone knew that the Russian soldiers had been ordered to cut off their patches and shoulder straps before they were sent to fight the Ukrainians (who'd suddenly lost their minds and joined up with the Americans). But since the TV was all hush-hush about our guys fighting in the Ukraine, I decided not to pry. I could appreciate the complexities of modern warfare and international politics. I'm not stupid.

"So you're, what?" I said. "A secret war hero?"

"Who cares if I am a hero?" he groaned, turning on his side. The TV remote fell to the floor, but he didn't pick it up. "My life is over."

"Your life is over?" I snatched the remote off the floor and laid it on the couch beside his hand. "Dude, you're only nineteen!"

Something crashed upstairs in our neighbor Krookin's flat, and our ceiling fixture lurched wildly. Boots hip-hopped the floor so hard, white flakes of ceiling plaster snowed down.

"Krookin is having a party again," I said, watching the fixture swinging over my brother's head. "Better move. That lamp fell three times while you were gone."

He didn't move, watching the cute lady on TV opening and closing her mouth. She was talking about snowfall, but you could hardly hear it because of the hip-hoppers upstairs. My brother squeezed all the volume out of the remote, but even at full blast, our wardrobe-sized TV (older than grandma) was no match for Krookin's subwoofers. With a groan, my brother lifted himself off the couch just enough to hurl the remote at the screen. He missed it. The remote smacked against the wall and cracked open, ejecting two tiny batteries.

"You're angry," I said. "That's good. Anger scares people. Why not ask Krookin for a job? His bodyguards are all war heroes like you, and he changes them all the time."

"Know why he changes them?" my brother said. "His bodyguards get killed. Gunned down in the bright of day on the streets of our capital."

He sat up so suddenly, I ducked. You never knew what he might do. He was often weird.

"I know what you're thinking," he said. "But you're wrong. I'm not afraid to die. I've been shot at by automatic weapons, grenades thrown at me, high explosives. I've been captured in a surprise attack, tortured by the enemy, but I kept my mouth shut the whole beautiful time until my unit bailed me out in a surprise counterattack. I'm not afraid, but I refuse to give Krookin the satisfaction of turning me down."

"How do you know he'd turn you down?"

"Because he would. He's been a jackass to me from kindergarten through high school. He'd be a jackass to me now."

I wasn't about to argue. I knew about jackasses. If not for the record snowfall that had shut down schools, they'd be dragging me out of the boiler room just about right now.

Krookin's front door was finished in bulletproof steel, heavily studded. When I stepped onto the doormat (it said "Not Welcome"), a security camera at the top of the doorframe

swung down at me. A siren went off. I leaped off the doormat and turned to run. The door banged behind me, and
someone caught the back of my collar and yanked me into
the hallway of the flat. The siren was louder there. Red
lights strobed. I dangled three feet from the floor, pinned
to the wall by Krookin himself.

"Hand it over!"

"Hand what over?"

He lifted me away from the wall and slammed me back
against it. "Don't be wise with me, worm. Let us have what
you were sent for."

"Don't you remember me?" I whined. "I live in the flat
below."

The strobe lights reflected off Krookin's mirror-shaven
head brighter than a disco ball. He looked like what he was
(dark shades, white sneakers, purple tracksuit with golden
zippers): a grown-up jackass. He blinked behind the shades
and took his hands off me. I went to the floor in a heap.

"Your mom's chandelier down again?" he said, annoyed
but not angry. A roll of bills packed thick as a snowball
appeared in his hand. "Get her a floor lamp." He peeled
one bill from the roll. "And don't bug me again. I'm busy."
He held the bill out for me to take (American dollars!), but
I surprised him. I didn't take the money.

"It's not about the chandelier. It's about my brother."

"Oh, yeah?" The roll of bills vanished, as if it was never there. "I didn't know he was back from the army." He looked into the security camera watching us from the wall and shouted, "Turn the damn thing off!" and right away the siren and the lights quit. "Was there a coming home party? I love your bro. He was my best bud at school. Did he tell you that?"

"Sure," I agreed. "He loves you, too."

"Oh, yeah?" He grinned ear to ear. (His teeth were capped in gold.) "Why don't you step into my office? We'll talk in private."

Every flat in our crumbling building was supposed to be a dead ringer. Three tiny, cramped rooms cramped together. Shabby, livable, and no one jealous. But Krookin must've scored the whole floor to himself. His hallway, plastered with mirrored wallpaper in black and gold, went on and on, zigzagging, with so many doors on either side, I lost count. I tried to peek into the room where the hip-hop was blasting from. "Don't go in there!" he snapped, and shoved me into his "office" (a dim yellow bulb, stacks of cardboard boxes, Chinese labels).

"I'm in the import-export business," he explained, slipping off his shades. "You take a little, you give a little, and everyone's happy." He had small, quick eyes that matched the color of his tracksuit. "So what is it about your brother? I'm all ears."

We sat on two boxes, facing each other, and I laid out my plan for him in detail. Since Krookin's bodyguards got killed all the time, which prevented them from staying on the job for long, he needed to hire my brother instead, a decorated war hero with loads of combat experience.

"Oh, yeah?" Krookin said. "He's got medals to show?"

I told him why my brother wasn't allowed to wear his medals.

"Secret missions?" he echoed after me. "Undercover?" And he burst out laughing so hard his gold teeth went ablaze in his mouth. "For the record," he said after he cooled off a bit, "nobody's killing my bodyguards. I fire them. Not my fault each one is dumber than the one before. I'd hire a smarty like your brother, but he lacks basic qualities required to carry protective duties."

"What are you talking about?" I protested. "He's got an AK-47 tattooed on his arm. Shed blood for Mother Russia."

Krookin bent his head to one side and looked at me, as if he was sorry that I was as dumb as his bodyguards. "Did he have that weapon inked on his arm in the service or after he'd come back home?"

"After I think."

"Here we go," he said, grinning. "For the record, most of the guys in our class were drafted, not just your brother, so I happen to have the inside scoop. He didn't go on no missions, and he's got no medals. I don't know why they even took him. He's blind as a bat. He spent two years in the kitchen."

"In the kitchen?"

"Yep. Serving soup."

I must have looked plenty heartbroken because he said, "I'm not saying he didn't want to bleed for Mother Russia; he just never had a chance."

"So why don't *you* give him a chance?" I said. "Show him some action?"

"Action?" Krookin laughed. "We used to drag him out of the boiler room at school where he was hiding from us. Your brother has never been much for action. He's not the type. How's he going to protect me and my valuables?"

I needed a little time to think it over, so I changed the subject. "How come you didn't go?"

"Go where?"

"To the army."

"Bad teeth." He tapped the gold in his mouth. "Dental implants adversely affecting the performance of duty."

In the end Krookin didn't offer the job. Instead, he proposed that my brother try out for one. Wasn't much of a tryout either—no action whatsoever, just some snow shoveling. Due to the record snowfall, Krookin's handsome pair of Mercedes-Benzes were buried under snow, and my brother was to dig them out and keep them running so that the engines wouldn't seize up in the cold.

I told my brother about Krookin's offer, and he made a big show of resisting, making up all kinds of goofy excuses why it was beneath him to try out. When finally he agreed to the tryout, he had to let me know that he was making an enormous sacrifice for *my* sake. Had I any idea just how eager he actually was, I'd have backed out of this snow-shoveling business before it spun out of control.

In no time I was hurrying after my brother down our crummy stairs (a homey mix of cabbage, stale cigarettes, and urine), dressed for warmth and felt-booted; he, camouflaged head to toe in his army fatigues. I carried under my arm the snow shovel that Krookin had entrusted to me, while my brother's shovel was slung over his shoulder, like a loaded AK-47.

When we arrived downstairs, he leaped up and kicked at the front door with his boot. The door didn't budge, but he landed on his back, hard.

I wished Krookin hadn't told me about my brother serving in the kitchen. A little embarrassed for his phony secret hero routine, I stepped around him and tried the door-knob. "Frozen solid," I said, "and probably snowed over on the outside, too."

"About face!" my brother hollered, jumping to his feet and marching back up the steps. I trooped after him to the second-floor landing, where a narrow window led out to the concrete awning above the front door. Our staircase did not have a back exit, so the only way out was through that window and scaling down the brick wall or jumping off the awning if the snowdrifts were deep enough. I didn't particularly like either option.

Summers, that window was kept open. The jackasses from my school, who also happened to live in our building, would lie atop the awning, waiting to spit on my head when I came out. With time they became sniper-sharp, and I took to wearing a hat folded out of our neighbor's newspaper.

My brother rattled the handle on the window frame. Nothing doing. The snow-plastered window was stuck. I sat on a step, watching him strain himself, suggesting from time to time better strategies until he snapped the handle clean off the window frame.

He said, "This is funny to you?"

Before I could explain that I wasn't laughing at him but at those jackasses never again spitting on my head from the awning (nothing broken gets fixed in our buildings, so the window was now shut forever), my brother shouted, "Step back!" and swung his shovel. I spun away, ducking from the flying glass.

At this point I should have headed back home. Were these not clear warnings: (1) Krookin banging me against the wall, and (2) my brother nearly slicing me to pieces with flying shards of glass? Obviously, the worst was yet to come, but did I go home? I did not.

"She wasn't kidding about the snow," my brother said when I climbed after him onto the awning.

"Who?"

"The weather lady on TV," he said. "A snowfall such as our Russian capital hasn't seen in one hundred and thirty years."

My shabby coat and threadbare scarf were no match for the record weather. It was bitter cold, and the snow was coming down thick and steady. The wind thrashed the snowflakes about, and when they huddled into snowdrifts, the wind churned them up into tornadoes. Because of that crazy wind, it looked as if the snow was coming down from above as well as rising from below. It was one white swirling hell.

"I'd rather be watching this on TV," my brother said.

"No kidding," I agreed. "How are we going to get down?"

My brother turned, squinting merrily at me behind his eyeglasses that were already touched with hoarfrost, smiled, and pushed me off the awning.

The problem with having an older brother is that it gives you a false sense of safety. In my mind he was to defend me against the jackasses—not be a jackass himself. I had only volunteered to help so I could keep an eye on him while he was pushing snow around. I didn't volunteer to be pushed around myself. Besides, he should've looked before he pushed me. The front door was snowed over, so I guess he figured there'd be snowdrifts below the awning. And there were except for one hard patch of icy dirt on which I crash-landed on my rear.

I heard him plow into a snowdrift a little way off, and in a moment, his face leaned over mine. He didn't have his glasses

"You're not hurt, bro?" he said.

"Oh, no," I said (ironically). "Thanks for giving me a hand."

In our building, Krookin was the only owner of four-wheeled vehicles, so even in this nasty blur it was no trouble finding his Benzes. Two large snowdrifts shaped like puffy cartoon cars sat side by side in front of the building.

"Bayonets!" my brother shouted. "Lunge!" And he thrust the blade of his shovel into the first snowdrift. I didn't know he had it in him, but he took to shoveling as murderously as if it were close combat. I never really got to try my hand at it—too busy ducking huge chunks of snow flying off his shovel. Soon my mouth, my nose, and behind my collar—all the way down to my long johns—were packed with snow. But he didn't seem to need my help. In no time, high-gloss sheet metal began to gleam through the patches of snow, a tinted windshield appeared, then seventeen-inch hubcaps, all-season tires. Presto, the first of the two Benzes stood before us like a black cutout in the snow.

"Guard!" my brother shouted. "Arms!" And he stood at attention, smartly holding the shovel at his side.

"Wow" was all I could say.

He smiled at me. "Why don't you start on the other vehicle, bro, while I finish up here?"

I said, "Sure," slung the shovel over my shoulder, and, stepping away from my brother, was instantly lost. The Benzes must've been parked not ten feet away from each other, but the snow was coming down so thick and fast you couldn't see through the blur. My hands went numb. My cheeks stung. The wind plucked me out of the snow and began tossing me about like a plastic bag. I called for my brother, but the wind snagged the words out of my mouth and drove them away. *Just don't go to sleep,* I said to myself. *If you fall asleep in the snow, you'll freeze to death.* Only I wasn't sleepy at all. I was scared.

Then something big lurched at me, or I lurched at it, I wasn't sure. So panicked, I couldn't tell at first. It turned out to be the second Benz buried beneath the snow. By then, I'd lost my shovel and my gloves. I thrust my bare hands into the snow where I figured the driver's door would be. I groped for the handle, found it, and pulled the door open. A massive lump of snow fell on my head from the roof of the car.

I collapsed into the driver's seat and shut the door. The dome light came on. A snowman in the rearview mirror spooked me, but it was only me looking at myself. My eyebrows and eyelashes were frosted, and under my carrot-colored nose, long strands of snot hung in yellow icicles. I dug the car key out of my snow-packed pocket and turned the vehicle on. The Benz purred like a tiger. I cranked up the heat and began melting. At once, the door came open.

"Are we allowed to do this?" my brother said. "You're dripping all over the interior."

"Get in," I said. "Thaw."

I could tell he didn't think it was a good idea, but he was cold and probably tired, so he told me to move over, slid into the driver's seat, and shut the door.

"Not much of a tryout, huh?" he said. "Shoveling snow?" He leaned over the steering wheel, squinting at the dashboard controls. "One sixty." He whistled respectfully and sat back, smiling. "Yep. I can live with that." He glanced at me quickly and, switching to his lazy voice, went on, "Of course, I'm used to fast driving. Drove a T-90 tank in the army. Once, they parachuted our machines smack in the middle of the enemy. I tell you, bro—that was something to behold. I was spinning in my tower, firing three sixty, bam, bam, bam! After, we chased what was left of 'em down the minefield." He made a sound of explosion and then grinned. "Yeah, me and my buddies, we've had our share of action."

I wondered for a moment if I was underestimating my school's jackasses. Would they really stop bullying me when they got a look at my brother? Could they not tell that underneath his army getup he was a phony warrior with a phony tattoo? True, he was good at shoveling snow, smashing windows, and tossing eleven-year-olds off high places, but was that enough to impress them?

The answer came unexpectedly in the form of a sharp

knock on the driver's-side window. My brother jumped. "What was that?"

We craned our necks at the window, but there was nothing there, just darkness and snowflakes.

"That was weird," he said.

Just then, the snow covering the windshield began to crack. A black glove burst through the snow, sweeping it aside. In the gap, a man in a knit black ski mask leaned close to the glass. The mask covered his entire head, with only two small round holes through which he peered at us for one creepy moment.

"What the—" my brother began, but the sight of the masked man darting toward the other Benz stopped him cold. The man climbed into the driver's seat, shut the door, and the Benz took off, churning up snow with its rear tires.

"Oh, no," I whispered. "He's stealing Krookin's car."

I looked at my brother slumped behind the steering wheel, squinting, lower jaw hanging loose in astonishment. I looked back through the windshield at the brake lights of the stolen vehicle flaring and disappearing behind the falling snow. I looked back at my brother.

"Hey," I said. "Do something."

When he didn't stir, I knew it was all over. Not only did he fail his tryout, but Krookin would probably kill him. With him dead, there'd be no one to defend me, so the jackasses at school would keep dragging me out of the boiler room and beating the daylights out of me until they killed me, too. I felt like weeping for our mother.

I turned away from my brother and began rocking my door back and forth to loosen the snow.

"What are you doing?" he whispered behind me.

"Go tell Krookin, what else?" I pushed at the door. "It's his car. Let him deal with it. You've had your share of action, right?"

I forced the door wide enough to get out, but just as I got a perch on the snowbank, a terrible roar sounded, and the Benz leaped forward. The door swung in reverse and knocked me back inside. I slid across the leather like a hockey puck, whacking my head on the edge of the console.

"Seat belt on!" my brother shouted. "Sit tight!"

I snatched at the seat belt, pulled it across my chest, and almost fit it into the lock when the Benz rocketed onto the street, shooting giant gobs of snow in all directions. The seat belt slipped from my hand and snapped me on the chin.

I guess my brother didn't have time to consider that the street in front of our building might be slippery. The Benz fishtailed, sliding on ice. He threw himself at the steering wheel, struggling to turn it or to keep it in place, I couldn't tell. My head was spinning. White smoke began billowing from under the wheels of our car, blocking whatever little I could see through the windshield. A sick feeling came over me, like it'd be a good idea to puke. I held it in until the white smoke cleared outside the windshield. It wasn't my head spinning at all. It was our car. We were going around and around in the middle of the intersection. The snow-drifts over the curbs, the corner bus stop, and a flashing traffic light kept whooshing by at even intervals. I puked on Krookin's leather armrest.

Too bad I'd missed seeing how my brother pulled us off that merry-go-round. Reality, such as it was, went dark for a little while. When I sat up, wiping bits of the scrambled eggs I'd had for breakfast off my chin, I saw Krookin's stolen Benz zipping along ahead of us.

"What are you going to do if you catch up with him?" I said. "He might be armed."

I could tell that my brother had no idea what he would do, but he said in his lazy voice, "Relax, bro—leave it all to me."

I looked at him leaning far over the steering wheel and squinting through the windshield.

"Glasses!" I screamed. "Where are your glasses?"

He glanced at me for just an instant, but long enough to plow into a snowdrift at the curb. The snowdrift exploded like a bomb. He spun the wheel wildly, and we were back on the road.

"Lost my specs," he said, "when we jumped off the awning."

"*You* jumped. I was pushed."

"That's how you parachute out of a chopper," he said. "They push you, ready or not."

"We were not in a chopper, okay?"

He turned to me, grinning, and opened his mouth to argue.

"Eyes on the road!" I shrieked.

He shrugged and went back to squinting through the windshield. How he could see anything at all, I didn't even want to know. On the windshield a terrible battle between the snow and the wipers was in progress. One pair of wipers fought an army of snowflakes diving into the glass like kamikaze pilots. The wipers were losing. Through the blur, the stolen vehicle's rear lights swam in and out of focus. No one, let alone a blind person like my brother, would dare drive in this weather. The streets were empty. We flew past the brightly lit storefronts, the neon signs, and under the red flashing traffic signals. Moscow looked like it did during New Year's—festive but a little sad, too. Like maybe it wanted to cheer up two wayward brothers before they'd soon perish in a fatal crash.

Then the thief swerved sharply and vanished into the dark. My brother's head popped up. "Where did he go?"

"The tunnel!" I shouted, wagging my finger at his window. "You missed it!"

He hit the brakes. I lurched forward, punching the dashboard with my forehead. The radio came on, and a hip-hop number exploded from the speakers. The bass, cranked up to the max, sledgehammered through my chest. My brother floored the gas in reverse, hit a divider, looped into a screeching U-turn, and we roared into the tunnel.

"This was my unit's battle song!" my brother shouted, nodding his head to the music. He knew the words, too. Stupid words about someone inked, armed, and dangerous, but it didn't stop him from bellowing them out. I glanced at the speedometer. He was doing about one-fifty. I thought of giving the seat belt another try, but there was no need. The speed squashed me deep into the baby-soft leather of my seat.

All in all, it wasn't too bad driving through the tunnel. There was no snow, the asphalt was dry, and it was superbright. Soon we were right on the stolen Benz's tail. Instead of numbers, its license plate said "KALASH."

"What's a kalash?" I shouted.

"Kalashnikov!" My brother nodded to his arm, where his tattoo was hidden below the army-issued layers. "AK-47!"

An AK-47 was an assault rifle—cheap to make, easy to use, and quick to fire. A fully automatic is able to unload about a hundred 39-millimeter rounds a minute. I remembered all this from kindergarten. Once, our kindergarten teacher invited a war veteran for an educational visit. He brought all kinds of guns for us to play with (not loaded). It made our teacher smile. I almost smiled too now, remembering. Back then, my brother was still halfway decent to me. When Mom was busy working, he used to walk me home from kindergarten.

"Hey," I shouted. "Remember how once you picked me up from kindergarten and bought me an ice cream cone?"

"What?" he shouted.

"Vanilla! Wasn't even my favorite, but that cone was the sweetest ever."

He turned and squinted at me. Our Benz felt my brother's lack of attention and swerved into the wall, crunching the side-view mirror. The driver's side went grinding against the concrete, scraping the high-gloss finish. Sparks flew. He spun the wheel to the right. The Benz shot diagonally across the road and smashed into the opposite wall. The right headlamp exploded.

Something walloped me on top of the head and slid heavily into my lap. I leaped back in panic, and the thing plunked into the puke on the floor and stood upright, leaning against my thigh. It was a Kalash. An AK-47. The gun was just as I'd remembered it from kindergarten, only this one was fancier. The stock and the guard were of shellacked wood, but all the metal parts were plated in gold, like Krookin's teeth. I looked up at a long narrow slot built into the roof of the car, just above the rearview mirror. The lid that had kept the gun from view was open now, swaying off its hinges. Three Velcro straps, ripped, hung loosely out of the slot.

I looked at my brother to check if he saw the gun, but he was too busy tearing the Benz away from the wall. He managed to cross onto the divider line, engine gunning. Weirdly, he seemed to be enjoying this. I wondered how bored he must've been in the army, scrubbing dishes in the kitchen all day, peeling potatoes, and serving soup to soldiers returned from battle, tired, shell-shocked, even wounded. Their lives meant something important; like shedding blood for Mother Russia for real, not inked in a phony tattoo.

I felt so bad for him that I lifted the AK-47 and shoved

it in front of his face. "Look!" I shouted. "This beats the kitchen, huh, bro? Better than serving soup!"

He spun around, gaped at me in shock, and saw the gun. "What?" I said. "What did I —"

"Soup?" he growled, grabbed the barrel of the gun, and tore it out of my hands. "I'll show you soup!"

His window slid down, and the wind roared into the car. My scarf was sucked into the opening, slapping my brother's face. Blinded, he spun the wheel, brakes screeching. I grabbed the armrests. He let go of the steering wheel, leaned out of the window, and began firing the AK-47 at the stolen vehicle.

Tra-ta-ta-ta-ta-ta-ta-ta-ta-ta-ta-ta-ta-ta-ta-ta ta-ta-ta!

Crazed with sudden freedom, our Benz went haywire, missing one wall, scraping the other, running straight down the yellow line before swerving again.

My brother ducked back inside the car—"Hold the wheel, idiot!"—and arched back out to shoot some more.

Had I ever learned to ride a bicycle (Mom never had money to buy one), I would've been more confident. Like a dog, the steering wheel smelled my fear and began yanking me every which way. There were other distractions besides. To my left, beyond the windshield, the barrel of the AK-47 was jumping up and down in my brother's hands, spitting flames out of its golden muzzle. Without his glasses, he was shooting up everything but the stolen vehicle. Long dotted lines of 39-millimeter holes sprouted in the vaulted ceiling. The overhead lights exploded one after another, leaving the tunnel dark behind us. I fought the steering wheel, crying to my brother to slow down, but he kept squeezing the gas pedal as hard as he was squeezing the trigger. His eye-hand-foot coordination was remarkable.

Gun blasting, hip-hop pounding, Benzes growling, we roared out of the tunnel. A wall of snowflakes walloped our windshield. The wipers kicked back into action. The brake lights of the stolen Benz bloomed bright red ahead, darting to the left, then to the right. One of our headlights was busted, and in the beam of the remaining light, I saw the stolen Benz fishtailing into a U-turn.

"Brake!" I screamed. "Brake now!"

My brother must not have heard me over the gunfire. We kept hauling at top speed toward the oncoming vehicle. I dropped the wheel and tried to yank my brother's boot off the gas. The car lurched sideways, and when I glanced above the dashboard, the headlights of the stolen Benz blinded me. I shut my eyes.

(Bye, Mom. I forgive you for never buying me a bicycle.)

There was a loud whine of tires, a thud, a shudder. The

engine choked and died.

I lay across the console, face squashed into the seat. My brother lumped on top of me. Were we dead? In the silence, I heard our Benz's engine ticking, cooling off. The leather stank from my puke. Chilled air blew in through the open window. I shivered, pleased that I could smell, feel, and hear, even after death, but then my brother stirred and began coughing.

"Get off me," I said.

He rolled off me, and I scrambled back into my seat. We looked at each other (not dead). We looked outside (nothing to see). The hood of our Benz was buried in snow to the windshield (we'd hit a snowdrift).

"I shot him dead for sure," my brother said.

"Oh, yeah?" I said. "Without your glasses? Where's the gun?"

He looked around, grinning stupidly.

Just then, his door flew open. "Come out with your hands up!" someone shouted. "Both of you!"

The man in the black knit ski mask stood silhouetted against the headlights of the stolen vehicle, aiming the gold AK-47 at us.

"Come out or I'll shoot!" he shouted. "Now!"

With our hands up, my brother and I climbed out

KALASH

through the driver's-side door. The thief looked at us for a moment, lifted the muzzle of the gun, and fired a burst into the falling snow. My brother and I ducked. The man exploded with laughter, lowered the gun, and ripped his mask off.

"Krookin?" my brother said, amazed. "What did you steal your own car for?"

Krookin's gold teeth sparkled. "Steal my car?" he managed to squeeze through the laughter. "What did you think your tryout was about? Shoveling snow?"

My brother glared at Krookin, and then he turned to me. "Put your hands down."

I put my hands down.

"You responded well," Krookin said. "The job you tried out for is known for its element of surprise. Your driving's good, but your shooting is lousy. You'll need some practice."

My brother started walking away.

"Where are you going?" Krookin said, confused. "You got the job."

"Are you coming or what?" my brother called to me over his shoulder, and kept walking.

I looked at Krookin. He stood under the falling snow, holding his shiny gun, his open mouth full of shiny teeth.

155

"I don't get it," he said to me. "He doesn't want the job?"

"I guess not." I ran after my brother.

"Krookin told you I served in the kitchen?" my brother said after I caught up with him. "What a jackass."

We walked for a while without talking. The snow was coming down hard. It was freezing.

"Want some ice cream?" my brother said.

"Now?"

The ice cream places were all closed, but a supermarket was open. My brother bought two vanilla sandwiches, and we ate them outside, shivering in the snow.

GENERAL POOPHEAD
BEING AN ACCOUNT OF THE
AFTERLIFE OF BENEDICT ARNOLD,
TRAITOR TO THE UNITED STATES
BY LAURIE HALSE ANDERSON

1. IN WHICH THE BOY WITH CLENCHED FISTS EMERGES FROM A NASTY PLACE

The wheel of time spun, and the bloodstained war ravens flew across the Forgotten Sea toward their appointment. When they reached the seven-masted Ship of the Darned, on that cursed voyage of lost souls, they landed, eager for what would happen next. Perched on the rigging, the war ravens stared down at the boulder that rested on the ancient deck: a giant lump of dried pelican poop.

One of the ravens chuckled. (It was pretty funny until you thought about how big the pelican must have been in order to deposit a turd the size of a recliner.)

Suddenly, an enormous wave made the ship buck and leap like a snake-bit horse. The giant poop boulder began to roll across the deck. The empty-eyed sailors dived out of the way while the ravens flapped their wings and croaked in excitement. The boulder crashed into the mainmast so hard that it cracked open like an old egg.

A boy tumbled out.

He looked to be about ten years old. He wore filthy pants that ended just below his knees, and a torn shirt that had last been seen in the American Colonies in 1752. He lay on the deck, looking more dead than alive, but if you had the sharp vision of a war raven, you could see his chest rise and fall.

An empty-eyed sailor dumped a bucket of seawater over the boy's head. The lad jumped to his feet, sputtering and wanting very much to say the worst words he knew but not being quite brave enough to say them. Instead, he clenched his fists.

"Why did you do that?" he yelled.

"You stink of pelican manure," said the empty-eyed sailor.

"I beg your pardon," declared the boy. "I do not—" He turned his head to smell his sleeve. "Oh, dear," he said. "That's disgusting."

"Indeed." The sailor yawned. "Do you remember your name, boy? Do you know why you're here?"

The boy narrowed his eyes in suspicion. Something was very wrong, but he couldn't figure out what it was.

"Of course I know my name, you dunderhead." The boy frowned. "It's, ah, it's a famous name. A worthy name, known all the world over. Just a moment, I, ah . . ."

He scratched at his head. 'Twas an alarming thing to wake up fresh-hatched from a massive pelican turd. It could make anyone forget his name for a while.

The empty-eyed sailor leaned on his mop. "Where do you come from?" he asked wearily. "Sometimes you remember that first."

"Connecticut," said the boy. "Everyone knows me there. I'm a smart lad, they say—strong and fearless."

"I heard you like a good fight."

"The only good fight is the one you win." The boy spat on the deck. "I almost always win." He wiped his mouth on his sleeve. "Tastes like something died in my mouth. Have I been sick?"

"You could say that." The empty-eyed sailor scrubbed

at the glistening loogie with his mop. "Concentrate, lad. What's yer name?"

"Same as my father's name, and his father before him." The dirty boy frowned again. "A proud name, to be sure. One of my forefathers was the royal governor of Rhode Island."

"You say that every blasted time," muttered the sailor. "I don't know why they keep trying."

"We come from a long line of distinguished Englishmen," continued the boy. "Father loved telling tales of their bravery, their cunning, and their gold."

"Did he tell them tales when he was drunk or when he was sober?" asked the sailor.

The boy glared. "Don't talk about my father that way."

The sailor shrugged. "I heard it from you in the first place, your last time here. Fond of the bottle you said he was. A terror to your mother."

The boy's shoulders slumped. "Aye, he was that," he said quietly.

For a moment the Forgotten Sea seemed to calm, and the fog began to lift. The boy took a cautious step backward, watching the expressionless sailors who limped around the deck and glancing at the curious unkindness of the ravens gathered above him. But then he scowled.

"What is this ship?" he demanded. "Where are we going? And why do you act as if you know me? I've never met you before."

The empty-eyed sailor gave a tired sigh. Being cursed to sail on the Forgotten Sea for an eternity is the most boring fate of all. "Remove your head from your hindquarters, young master, and pray tell me your name."

"Does he remember yet?" called one of the ravens.

All over the ship the empty-eyed sailors shivered at the sound of the war raven's voice.

"Hurry up, lad," said the sailor with the mop. "Them gods are waiting."

"Gods?" The boy clenched his fists tighter. "What are you talking about? Are you daft, old man?"

The empty-eyed man spat out a string of words that sailors like to use when they are angry, then he said, "You'll never learn, will you? No matter how many times we go through this. Waste of bloody time, if you ask me." He thought about his miserable fate and sighed again. "Which they never will."

The fog, which had been keeping a respectful distance, rushed at the ship.

"What's your name?" The empty-eyed sailor's voice had turned angry. He stepped toward the boy and suddenly seemed to be made of iron and rage instead of rags and sadness.

"Is that fog . . . red?" the boy asked, shrinking a bit from the sailor. He gave his head a shake. "Can't be," he muttered to himself. "There's no such thing as red fog or a fog that smells of death."

The ravens on the rigging screamed. The fog rolled in faster.

The empty-eyed sailor roared. "What! Is! Your! Name?"

A wave of fear jolted the boy's memory. "Benedict," he cried. "My name is Benedict Arnold." He stared at his fists. "I'm a soldier, I think. Or I will be a soldier. Or I was, a long time ago." He looked up as the bloodstained war ravens on the rigging flapped their wings. "What's happening to me?"

That's when the ravens descended upon the boy in a terrible storm of feathers and beaks and plucked him from the deck.

2. IN WHICH THE BOY WITH THE CLENCHED FISTS BECOMES THE BROKEN HERO

The ravens surrounded young Benedict in a tornado of black feathers, then carried him down the stairs, level after level after level. (This was a cursed ship, remember, with dark magic lurking everywhere. The inside of the ship was much larger than the outside could possibly contain.)

Once deep below, the birds dropped him to the floor-boards with a thud. The boy who had been ten years old above deck now appeared as a man of some thirty years, dressed in a Continental uniform with tarnished buttons and muddy boots. He stood slowly and limped a few steps, for one leg was now shorter than the other, and it pained him terribly. Holding his head in his hands, he spoke to himself. "Must have fallen from my horse. I've gone all muzzy-headed, thinking myself a boy at sea again."

"Benedict." A low and dangerous voice called his name. A woman's voice.

He slowly raised his head, peered into the gloom, and gasped. He was standing in an enormous hall, warmed by fireplaces large enough to drive an oxcart through. The air smelled of cooking meat, gunpowder, and the stench of people who have gone years without a bath. A long table stretched the length of the hall, crowded with chairs and covered by bleached bones, overturned mugs, and rock-hard crusts of bread. Candles flared and guttered on the table and along the dark walls.

The war ravens soared along the high ceiling, circled

the hall three times, then—to the amazement of Benedict Arnold—one by one their wings turned into arms, their tails folded and joined with their legs, their beaks retracted into noses, and their feathers turned into clothes. Thus, most of them transformed into their oldselves. A few turned into wolves, one took on the shape of a lean octopus, and the last became a gray rat the size of a walrus.

These were the ancient gods of war, from nearly every culture and almost every age. No matter how many reminders were sent out, a few gods always mixed up the meeting dates or got sidetracked by a battle or an old-fashioned nose punching contest that would lead to years of bloodshed and thousand of corpses until no one could remember why they started fighting. But all things considered, it was an impressive showing that filled most of the seats around the council table. The crimes of Benedict Arnold were the worst sort. Judging him was serious work.

The gods of war sat down and reached for mugs suddenly filled with ale and for plates that overflowed with fresh-roasted meat.

Benedict blinked. He knew that these were gods without being told, and he knew that they'd come to judge him. But he did not know how he could understand such a thing. He felt his head for lumps. *I've been knocked about by some scoundrels,* he thought. *Or mayhaps this is a fever dream. But if this truly is happening, then I must leave immediately.*

Keeping his eyes on the feasting gods, he slowly limped toward the stairs, thinking to get back to the main deck.

The largest man at the long table, the one who most resembled a craggy mountain, suddenly appeared in front of Benedict. The man raised his hairy arm and pointed, motioning for Benedict to stand in front of the largest fireplace, where all could observe him. A woman stepped from the shadows and met him there. She was tall and powerful, a warrior with glowing eyes, beautiful and horrifying at the same time.

"Benedict," she repeated.

She's a Valkyrie, thought Benedict, *a spirit of carnage,* though again, he didn't know how or why he knew that.

"Welcome back," the Valkyrie said. Her voice sounded like a sharp blade scratching upon a gravestone. "This court is now in session."

"Court?" Benedict snapped. "This is no court; it's witchcraft."

"Not at all, General," she said. "You have been brought before the gods of war to answer for your crimes."

"Balderdash," Benedict spat. "I'm not staying for this

167

nonsense." He turned toward the stairs again, but found he could not move his legs. His feet had sunk into the floorboards, up to his ankles. He swallowed hard and thought fast. "Have I been arrested for dueling? A tavern brawl? Surely the gods of war can't object to a good fight. Can they?"

"Don't try to be funny, you fool," warned the Valkyrie. "It never works here."

"Where is here?" Benedict held up his hands and looked around the strange hall. "I wake up as a smelly boy, I turn into this me after being assaulted by birds that are not birds, and now I'm held fast in this impossible place where I know things I can't know."

The Valkyrie winced, as if she were developing a terrible migraine and just wanted to take a nap on a soft bed. She rubbed her forehead. "They keep promising me that one of these times you'll remember everything. I'm beginning to think it'll never happen." She smoothed her hair and studied Benedict. "You're mostly dead, you nitwit. Been that way for hundreds of years, as your people measure such things."

Benedict frowned. "Mostly dead?"

"Not fully dead yet because neither Heaven nor Hell will let you in. Because of your crimes, you've been cursed to travel on the Ship of the Darned, to contemplate your misdeeds. Whenever the wheel of time turns, you're given another trial and a chance to repent. The gods of war are much nicer than most people realize."

"They entombed me in pelican poop," Benedict pointed out.

"Think of it as a spa treatment." A weathered scroll appeared in the Valkyrie's hands. "Let's get this over with. During the American Revolution you bravely led a command of more than a thousand men through hundreds of miles of winter wilderness to Quebec."

"I did," Benedict said in a clear voice. "The weather prevented us from taking the city, but it still counted as a success. Thomas Jefferson told the Continental Congress of my great deeds."

"You were wounded?"

"Shot in the leg."

"And you were promoted because of your valor and sacrifice?"

Benedict paused. "Jealous officers schemed against me and denied me the rank I was owed."

The gods of war muttered a bit. Petty infighting was a common problem in all armies.

The Valkyrie glanced at her scroll. "You later defied

orders and led the charge that determined the American victory at Saratoga."

Several gods cheered.

Benedict nodded his appreciation of their support. "A glorious day. I rode a magnificent horse straight at the enemy's guns. My courageous example rallied my men, and they followed me into victory."

"Hmmm," said the Valkyrie. "And you were shot again."

"In the same leg." Benedict frowned. "While I was bleeding and near death in a hospital, other men took credit for my actions. They stole my glory and my chance of advancement."

"Your leg kept you from leading a command, so you were appointed military leader of Philadelphia. You used that position for your own profit, thus robbing from both your army and your country."

"You should throw pelican poop at Congress," Benedict said bitterly. "After sacrificing my body and my fortune, I was mistreated by those dogs. They ruined me, and then they ruined the country."

"You were accused of misusing your powers."

"Not true!" shouted Benedict. "I did no more than countless others. But I was the one they picked on. I was the one made to suffer shame."

The Valkyrie sighed deeply. "Yeah, yeah, yeah. If they were treating you so badly, why did they put you in charge of West Point? They made you responsible for thousands of soldiers."

Benedict shrugged. "They could not deny my brilliance."

"They trusted you," said the Valkyrie. "What did you do with their trust?"

Benedict did not answer.

"You tried to sell out the soldiers under your command." The Valkyrie's voice grew louder. Indeed, she grew larger and stronger as her anger flared. "You prepared to hand over the army at West Point to the British."

Low growls came from the gods in wolf form.

Benedict's heart stuttered. "You see, the other generals never appreciated my gifts," he said. "They were jealous of—"

"You abandoned the cause of your country," she continued. "You pissed on the men you were supposed to lead. You spit on the land of your fathers. Admit it!"

The stench of blood was thick in the air. Swords, axes, knives, guns, and large rocks appeared on the table. The restless gods of war were itching for a fight.

The Valkyrie shrieked in a voice of a thousand flaming

eagles. "Are you a traitor, Benedict Arnold?"

"Yes," whispered the broken hero.

3. IN WHICH THE BROKEN HERO TURNS COAT AND MAKES EXCUSES

"But if the British had only listened to me," he added, "they could have won. I had great plans, the knowledge and the courage. I could have changed everything. I could have made it great!"

When the Valkyrie spoke again, her voice was dead calm. "You sold out your brother-soldiers and your country, and now you stand there sniveling because you didn't like the way things turned out?"

Benedict Arnold bowed his head.

The mountain-shaped god slowly rose to his feet. The other gods regarded him with surprise, for no one could remember the last time he spoke.

"Why?" he asked, small flames curling out between his teeth. "Why did you betray your friends?"

Time paused. The other gods sat motionless. Waves on the Forgotten Sea froze in mid-swell, and the ship ceased rocking. The hearth fire and candle flames stood still as Benedict Arnold, adrift on the cursed ship, was forced to answer this most awful question.

A great bead of sweat dropped from his forehead and onto the table. He did not want to answer it.

"Well?" demanded the Valkyrie.

Benedict Arnold lifted his head. The angry young soldier had vanished. In his place stood a withered old man, his face deeply lined with disappointment, his hands twisted with age. Instead of a uniform, he wore a shabby coat and fraying pants. He was missing most of his teeth.

"The British gave me a commission," he said. "Gave me troops to lead."

"You already had troops to lead, American troops," observed the Valkyrie. "Did they promise to make you king of the united Colonies?"

Benedict shook his head.

"Did they offer to marry you to a princess?"

"Already had a wife and children," Benedict said.

"You took them with you to England, did you not?"

"Aye," Benedict said quietly.

"Did the English people hail you as a hero? Did they throw flowers at your feet, grant you castles, erect statues in your honor?"

Benedict muttered something under his breath. The mountain-sized god leaned forward, a hand cupped behind his ear, and grumbled in irritation.

"I said no, they did not," Benedict repeated louder, lifting his chin. "But I had the respect and admiration of the king and his councillors."

The enormous rat giggled.

"King George, the Mad King, called you a disgusting worm," said the Valkyrie.

The gods of war murmured, nodding in agreement.

"He did not!" protested Benedict. "I walked with King George! I walked by his side and explained the mistakes made by his generals. The king respected me!"

"Worm! Worm! Worm!" the gods chanted, beating the table with their fists.

"Stop it!" shouted Benedict. "It wasn't fair! They never gave me the money they promised!"

All noise stopped.

The Valkyrie picked up a shard of bone from the floor and used it to pick a bit of gristle from her teeth.

"Do you repent?" she asked quietly. "Do you wish you could apologize to the country and the people whom you sold for a small bag of silver?"

"No!" declared Benedict. "I was right! If they'd listened to me, I could have won it all. They would have crowned me with glory instead of shame. It wasn't fair, none of it!"

"Worm!" the gods of war roared. "Worm! Worm! Worm!"

A few of the gods started banging on the table with their weapons. The noise made dust rain from the ceiling. An ax flew across the table (no way to tell if that was an accident or not), and shouting erupted. A few more sharp-bladed weapons followed as words spoken in all the languages of time turned into the shrieks and caws of war ravens. The fog of battle had returned, soaking through the walls with the sharp tang of bloody fear.

Old Benedict shifted his weight off his bad leg and grimaced. How many more centuries would he have to suffer this torment? He weakly slapped the table. "It wasn't fair," he whispered.

"Time to go up top," said the Valkyrie. "Time for the Judgment."

4. IN WHICH THE ALMIGHTY PELICAN OF JUDGMENT DROPS THE VERDICT OF THE COURT UPON THE TURNCOAT

The walk up the stairs was longer and harder than coming down them had been. A third of the way up, Arnold unaged and became a thirty-year-old soldier again. After climbing many more flights, he returned to being a lad of ten. His back was straight and tall, his wounded leg had healed, and his heart was mostly pure. But his soul was still stained with his crimes and polluted with his lack of remorse.

The gods of war drifted up the stairs, some in raven form, others retaining arms, legs, and bits of humanness that combined into hideous shapes that delighted them as they took their places on deck and on the rigging. Somewhere a single drum beat loudly.

The wind gusted, blowing curtains of fog across the deck. Young Benedict Arnold shivered and clenched his fists.

The wind blew again, ruffling the sails rhythmically, like bellows, or the regular breath of a giant. The clouds parted.

The Almighty Pelican of Judgment flapped into sight.

Benedict groaned.

The gods cheered.

The Ship of the Darned rocked violently on the churning waves, and the boy fell to his knees. He pounded the deck with his fists. "It's not fair!"

The Almighty Pelican of Judgment, a creature somewhat larger than a T. rex and a bit smaller than a blue whale, swooped over the ship, sighted the target, and twitched her tail feathers to the side. A waterfall of pelican poop rained on the head of the guilty, silencing him. The soldier who had betrayed his country and his oath collapsed under the weight of the smelly goo and officially became a living turd.

"Benedict Arnold," muttered an empty-eyed sailor. "General Poophead."

The gods of war faded into the fog, laughing with grim satisfaction. Some were called to their work in the present age, others traveled to long ago or to an age yet to come. The Valkyrie signed the court transcript in blood and melted into the mist, still dreaming of a nap. The empty-eyed sailors refilled their buckets and returned to the endless task of swabbing the deck.

One of them whistled "Yankee Doodle."

THE WARRIOR
AND THE KNAVE
BY INGRID LAW

"If you're going to complete this perilous undertaking, young man, you'll need the right tools and weapons."

Yes! I barely restrain myself from pumping my fists in the air. Somehow I manage to hold my arms motionless where I stand. I'm pretty sure I look more dignified this way. More like a real hero in the making. Mom always says I don't know the meaning of the word "motionless." She rolls her eyes when she says it, too, like it's a bad thing. But you know how parents can be—teachers, too—always blowing things out of proportion.

My parents and teachers are far, far away now. Mom, Dad, Coach Fulton . . . they won't have a clue where to start looking when they discover me missing. How could they? I don't even know where I am! Who'd ever guess that Allie Chen keeps a crazy, sucking black-hole vacuum-vortex thingy hidden in the back of her locker, right behind her coat and a poster-board collage of pig pictures? Long-tailed pigs, short-tailed pigs, pigs with curly tails. There are even pigs with cartoon speech bubbles that say "Wee-wee-wee" . . . and so on.

Note to self: As soon as you return to reality, Wendell, ask Allie why she likes pigs so much—and why she has a crazy, sucking BLACK-HOLE VACUUM-VORTEX THINGY inside her locker.

I turn my attention back to the old woman who's been talking to me. It's her quaintly thatched cottage I'm currently standing in, her garden and world I've so recently landed in, after getting sucked through the back of Allie's locker. This woman—she told me to call her "Mother," which seems all kinds of wrong and creepy—is dressed like she's about to march in a Thanksgiving Day parade: funny black hat, long woolen dress, old-fashioned shawl. She has downy hair, and small eyes that are a bit too close together. She also has the most impressive nose I've ever seen; it's practically a beak.

"I was expecting the *girl*," says Mother. "But I suppose

you'll do." She squints at me like she is sizing me up. Or like she's trying to decide what I'd taste like chopped into bite-size pieces and baked inside a pie, along with some plums and a few blackbirds, maybe.

"The girl promised she'd return as soon as she finished battling the Gee-Omma Tree," says Mother. "Did the villainous tree defeat her? Has she perished?"

"Er . . . do you mean Allie?" I ask. "Allison Chen? I'm pretty sure she's fine. I think she's got world history now, not math. But *I'm* here, and, *ahem*, you said something about weapons?" I waggle my eyebrows meaningfully.

Mother nods and shuffles away from me. She moves toward a large cabinet on the far side of the parlor. I'm beginning to like this room. Here, Mother has already served me cake and told me exactly why she needs a champion like me.

Let me repeat: *a champion like me.*

She really said that.

No one has ever thought of me as a champion before. Not in the entire history of my life. Not even last week, after I spent four straight days of spring break searching unsuccessfully for Mrs. Finkleman's missing dog, Mr. Sixpence.

I think I've grown an inch or two just by being around

this old lady and her insanely misplaced confidence in me. My jeans definitely feel shorter and less baggy. My Grandville Middle School Warriors T-shirt is probably getting all stretched out from the pride ballooning in my chest. If this keeps up, Mom and Dad might not even recognize me when I get home.

If I get home?

Nope. Nuh-uh. I will definitely be going home soon. Right after I knock this whole hero thing out of the ballpark.

I squeak a little and jump back as four gray mice zip past me. One mouse scampers up the side of a grandfather clock in the corner, then runs down the other side again, just as the clock gongs a single chime. The three remaining rodents scurry around the room crazily. They bump into the furniture. Into one another, too. Like they can't see where they're going. I'm unable to decide if this is entertaining, sad, or a little bit disturbing. But as Mother unlocks the cabinet, I forget about the mice and allow myself to pump my fist in the air, just once.

You know how there's that moment in some fantasy stories when the main character is presented with the Hammer of Whosit, or pulls the Great Sword of Whatsit from a big rock, or finds the magical bow of the Lost

Warrior of Wherever? And then, not long after, through a series of bruising trials, the young hero becomes the next Triple-Awesome Champion Deluxe of All Time, even though they're only eleven, twelve, maybe thirteen years old? They might only be able to do one push-up. They might only have a friend group of two (on a good day). But invariably, a fantasy hero always gets to transform into the champion no one ever believed they could be. Not even themselves.

Dude. I *love* those kinds of stories.

I *am* that gangly, awkward twelve-year-old nobody. I have all the qualifications. Back home, in Grandville, I currently have a friend group that teeters precariously between one and zero, depending on whether Jay Gupta is talking to me or not. And Coach Fulton merely shakes his head whenever I celebrate the completion of one epic chin-up by dancing the funky chicken. So now that I face the prospect of a completely unforeseen fantasy-hero type situation—of getting my very own enchanted weapons . . . *me*, Wendell James MacDougall-Flowers—I am psyched. I am over the moon. I am jumping-up-and-down, peeing-my-pants-with-excitement *thrilled*.

My skin prickles as the tall cabinet door creaks open. Dust motes hover around me, illuminated by a single sunbeam that spears the room. Stepping into the light, I find myself bouncing on my toes a little. Shaking out my arms. Trying to stay loose the way athletes do. I can't believe any of this is happening. No more than forty minutes have passed since Cameron Jamison stuffed me into Allie's locker in the abandoned seventh-grade hallway.

I was in school, then—*SHHHLOCK!!*—I was here, in some mysterious, distant world, being told I'm a warrior. Being asked to save the day.

Maybe I'll get some armor, too, I think. *And a cape! A cape would rock.*

Picturing myself decked out in broad-shouldered battle gear, I don't hold back. This time I pump *both* fists in the air, adding a tiny hop.

"Your enemy is a contemptible bandit and a ruffian," says Mother as she rummages through the cabinet. Things clatter, clunk, crash, thunk, before . . .

"Bingo!" she says triumphantly. "I've found just what you'll need to go up against the Knave."

According to Mother, the Knave has been harassing people, stealing their stuff, and generally acting like a colossal monkey fart for some time now, making the residents of Mother's world colossally miserable. This kid stole Mother's only goose, and now she wants it back. I don't

THE WARRIOR AND THE KNAVE

really know what the big deal is. I mean, it's a *goose*, not a Nintendo 3DS or something. But when a guy gets called upon to help, he helps. Right?

I straighten up, standing taller in my sunny spotlight. I am ready. Ready to receive my new weapons with pride and—

What the freaking fish sticks? My jaw drops as Mother steps out of the shadows and shoves a jumble of objects into my arms without fanfare: a pie tin, a shepherd's crook, and an empty burlap bag barely big enough to hold a shoebox. It is a disappointing turn of events. What kind of a hero carries a *pie tin*, a *shepherd's crook*, and an empty *burlap bag*?

"Er . . . what exactly do you expect me to do with *these*?"

Mother observes the droop in my shoulders and hoists one tufty eyebrow. "Are you sure you're up for this, young Wendell? Perhaps I'd better wait for the girl to re—"

"No!" I quickly cut her off. "I am totally up for this, I swear. I mean . . . I just . . . I'm going up against the *Knave*, right? Shouldn't I have a sword or something? You know. Just in case?"

"In case of what?" asks Mother.

"Er . . . trouble?"

"Be assured, my boy," Mother replies solemnly, sticking

her big, beaky nose in my face. "There will most definitely be trouble."

Before I leave the cottage, Mother fills my burlap bag with some provisions: an apple, some cheese, and an egg salad sandwich big enough to feed all the king's men *and* their horses. I watch her do this. And yet, when she hands the bag back to me, it's empty. Though the bag itself seems somewhat bigger than it first appeared.

"What the—?"

"It's enchanted, of course." Mother dismisses my astonishment with a wave. "The bag grows to hold whatever you need. But it will never get any heavier, and you won't ever be able to see or feel anything you've placed inside it. So you'll have to *remember*." She knocks her knuckles twice against my forehead. "In order to get what you need from it, you'll have to speak the name of the thing you want, backward. But heed this warning, young Wendell! Don't ever reach into the bag! If you do, you'll be drawn inside and trapped forever—unless someone says *your* name backward to get you out."

"Backward?"

"Try putting that shepherd's crook in there and see what happens," instructs Mother.

I look at the long, hooked staff. "It's way too big."

Scowling, Mother raps her knuckles against my skull again, harder this time. It's clear she's having second thoughts about her new champion. "Haven't you been listening?"

Heat rushes to my cheeks. I don't want Mother to think she's chosen the wrong person for the job, just because I can't figure out how to operate a magic bag. Allie Chen would probably catch on quicker. She's pretty smart, even if she does have an obsession with pigs and hates geometry. She won top honors at this year's science fair with her project "The Many Uses of Manure." That's when Cameron Jamison started picking on her almost as badly as he picks on me. Though, as far as I know, Cameron hasn't ever stuffed Allie in a locker before, just to keep her from telling on him for stealing her stuff.

I set down my pie pan and stick one end of the shepherd's crook into the bag.

"Corn nuts on a cracker!" I cry when the staff immediately gets sucked into the bag and disappears. I regard the burlap sack with new respect. It is now five times longer than it was before—the same length as the staff, in fact—yet it still looks and feels completely empty.

"Now get it out again," says Mother, clearly trying to be a patient instructor.

Remembering what she said about saying names backward, I retrieve the bag and stare into its empty shell.

Thinking hard for a moment, I rearrange letters in my head and sound them out. Then I shout: "KOORC!" Which comes out sounding a lot like "cork." But it must be correct, because the wooden staff rockets out of the bag and hits me squarely between the eyes, knocking me on my butt and making little twinkle-twinkle stars flash like diamonds all around me.

"Eh, well. You'll get the hang of it soon enough," says Mother. "Just remember, young Wendell. You possess all the tools and weapons a hero needs most. Employ them! Use your brain! Use your heart! Use the gifts you've been given!"

Staring at the pie pan and the shepherd's crook, I am completely mystified by my so-called "gifts." At least the magic bag is cool.

"Are these enchanted, too?" I ask hopefully, holding up the pie pan and the crook.

"Don't be ridiculous," she says, clucking her tongue. And before I can ask anything more, she pushes me out her front door, not even offering me an ice pack for the lump on my forehead.

Turns out, having a magic bag is a truckload of fun. As I walk mile after crooked mile, headed in the direction of the Knave's not-so-secret enclave—which, according to

Mother, is only a few hours to the west, across a river and past a fork in the road, at the foot of Fiddle Peak—I start putting anything and everything that's not nailed down inside the burlap sack. I want to know if there's a limit to what the bag can hold. So far, there isn't. I've collected a bunch of stones. Some small, others the size of my head. I've also picked up fat sticks and skinny sticks, and about forty-seven pinecones. But no matter how many things I put inside the bag, it never gets any heavier.

The bag does continue to get bigger, though, and soon, I have the thing wrapped around and around my neck like a scarf, even though it's scratchy and warm in the afternoon sun.

I continue to carry both the crook and the pie pan in my hands; somehow it doesn't feel right to store them in the bag. To make myself feel less dorky, I pretend they are the epic weapons I'd been hoping for: the Noble Staff of Wendell! The Unbreakable Shield of the MacDougall-Flowers Clan! Clearly, this might be equally dorky, but it helps me feel better nonetheless. I may be in the seventh grade, but I'm still pretty good at make-believe.

I thump the pie pan against my leg as I walk, trying to figure out how a round metal pan could be useful for anything but baking. I suppose it *could* make a stellar Frisbee. . . . I throw the pan a few times to test out this idea. I miss every rock and tree I aim for. But that's nothing new.

The shepherd's crook is heavy, yet it makes a decent walking stick. It might also be good for conking a bad guy on the head, I suppose, or for tripping somebody, or getting a kite out of a tree.

Feeling my stomach rumble, I open my bag, consider carefully for a minute, then say: "ELPPA!" This time, I'm ready to grab the object that whizzes toward me. "And the crowd goes wild!" I shout, hopping up and down with my arms above my head, as if I just made a game-winning catch.

Munching on my apple, I continue to follow the path Mother set for me. In an attempt to keep my anxiety in check, I keep my mind busy by figuring out how to say all kinds of things backward. So far, I've come up with:

EVANK

ESOOG

NOREMAC

SD3 ODNETNIN

It isn't long before I hear the sound of rushing water. I step up my pace, eager to get my confrontation with the Knave over and done with. Then I can bask in the glory of a job well done and find my way home to Grandville.

190

But when I reach the river and see the water leaping over the rocks, I momentarily forget my nervousness. I rub the coarse, loosely woven fibers of the burlap bag between my fingers. Then I dip my hand into the icy water. "Hunh," I grunt. "This could be interesting."

Would it work? *Could* it work?

Curious, I remove the burlap bag from around my shoulders, roll up my pants, kick off my socks and shoes, and wade into the water.

I open the mouth of the bag, allowing the river to flow directly into it. I watch the bag grow . . . and grow . . . and *grow.*

When I slog back out of the water again, the bag is still completely empty, as usual. It is also 100 percent dry *and* the size of a bedsheet.

"Hunh," I grunt again. "I think that might have worked."

I tie the bag back around my neck, this time letting it drag on the ground behind me. When I catch sight of my shadow, it looks exactly like I'm wearing a cape.

"Yes!" I shout over the sound of the river. "This almost makes up for me not getting a sword."

After I cross the river, I set my sights on Fiddle Peak and refuse to be distracted. I mean, if I want to get Mother's goose back and save the day, I'd better stay focused, right? Though I do pause briefly when I meet a girl who's searching for some wayward sheep; but I'm on the road again as soon as I help her find them. I'm also traveling lighter now, because I gave the girl my shepherd's crook. She obviously needed one, and I'm no jerk. Besides, I have other tools at my disposal.

Eventually, I come to the fork in the road, and I strike out through fields and farmland. With my burlap cape billowing majestically behind me, I blaze a path between the two roads, just as Mother instructed . . . until the overpowering stench of manure stops me short, making my eyes water.

I plug my nose and fan myself with the pie pan as I contemplate the pig farm in the distance. I imagine how happy Allie would be if she were here. There are long-tailed pigs, short-tailed pigs, pigs with curly tails . . . not to mention tons and tons of raw material for more prize-winning science fair projects.

Something clicks inside my brain, and I pause to consider for a moment, trying to use my gray matter the way Mother ordered me to before I left her house. Call me crazy, but even though the stink here is almost unbearable, I decide it might be worth my while to linger for a bit. And maybe collect a few things into my bag.

When I eventually do walk on, nearly twenty minutes pass before I realize I forgot my pie pan back at the farm. But there's no going back. The sun is low in the sky. I've got to keep moving. By now, my mom and dad have probably convinced the Grandville Police Department to issue a missing-kid alert. If nothing else, I'm going to be in serious trouble for not calling to check in.

The Knave's enclave is not what I expected. I thought I'd find the guy standing at the top of a tall tower or hiding behind some impenetrable fortress. Instead, I'm looking at a small warehouse built in the shadows at the base of Fiddle Peak. The front door is propped open with a brick, yet there are hand-painted signs everywhere that say things like "Get Lost!" and "Go Away!" and "Mine, Mine, ALL MINE!"

"You only have to grab Mother's goose and get out again, Wendell," I tell myself. And, taking a deep breath, I slip through the open door without knocking.

Turns out, the Knave isn't just a thief and a bully, he's a hoarder.

I make my way slowly through a towering maze of rubbish inside the warehouse. Piles of pilfered belongings reach as high as my eyeballs and past my head, sometimes all the way to the ceiling. There are hundreds of mismatched dishes and spoons, pipes and bowls. Heaps of candlesticks, bags of wool, and oodles of decaying pumpkin shells lay everywhere. I steer clear of a collection of cooking pots that look and smell like they're filled with nine-day-old porridge.

I'm super-surprised when I stumble into a teetering stack of board games. Wait. *Board games?* I'm even *more* surprised to discover that the Knave has a mountain of video games, game consoles, and controllers, too. These all feel completely out of place here. They twist a sharp corkscrew into my sense of what's real and what's not real.

I pick up an old GameCube controller and turn it over.

"Didn't you read my signs?" A surly voice ruptures the stillness inside the warehouse, making me jump. "My signs that say 'No Touchy!' and 'Stay Out'?" The questions are punctuated by the yap of a small dog, whose bark sounds strangely like laughter—and also strangely familiar. The barking is immediately followed by a loud honk from somewhere farther back in the building.

The goose!

I drop the ancient controller and turn around.

Sitting sideways in a high-backed chair positioned atop

a platform built of thousands of seventh-grade textbooks is a thick-necked kid not too much older than I am. His legs are draped lazily over one arm of his chair, and he leans against the other. A curly white dog perches on a pillow below him, simultaneously growling and wagging its tail.

Necklaces, chains, and medals dangle from the top of the Knave's throne-like seat while all around it sit trophies: basketball, baseball, ballroom dancing, you name it. Strangely, these are all things from *my* world, just like the video game components, the board games, and the textbooks.

A large silver tray rests on the kid's stomach. The tray is covered in pastries—mostly tarts, I think. And he's got a half-eaten tart in his hand.

Another honk echoes through the maze of junk.

"Are you the Knave?" I ask, stepping boldly forward, trying not to fidget, bounce, or twitch.

The kid studies me for a moment, chewing with his mouth open, spewing crumbs. He takes in my burlap-bag cape—which is now the biggest and coolest it's ever been—and smirks. Then he shrugs and cleans some powdered sugar from his hand by wiping his fingers on his fancy pants and ruffled shirt. It's clear he doesn't see me as an epic force to be reckoned with.

"Some people call me the Knave, yes." He shrugs again. "*I* call me a self-starter, a guy who takes what he wants. Would you like a tart?" He holds up the tray of pastries. "I'll have my maid prepare some tea. Polly!" he calls out. "Put the kettle on, Polly! We've got company." Then he snorts. "Just kidding. I don't have a maid. AND I DON'T EVER, *EVER* SHARE MY THINGS!" The Knave's expression turns dark as both his mood and his volume shift dangerously without warning.

I suddenly worry that I'm standing in the presence of a psychopath. Mother didn't say anything about the Knave being totally unhinged.

The kid throws the silver tray at me. I jump back and watch it clatter to the floor; delicious-looking tarts fly everywhere. The dog leaps toward the fallen pastries but is brought up short by a leash tethered to the leg of the Knave's chair.

"I'm not here for tea," I say loudly, hoping I sound ten times braver than I actually feel. "I've come to retrieve a certain goose you stole from a certain old woman who likes to be called Mother." I hope this declaration doesn't make *me* sound unhinged.

The Knave rolls his eyes and tosses the last bite of his tart in the dog's direction. It lands just beyond its reach.

Then he stands, rubbing his hands together slowly, brushing away crumbs—or getting ready for a fight. It's kind of hard to tell the difference. The little dog barks its funny bark and strains against its leash, trying to reach the discarded bite of tart.

I wonder if the Knave stole the dog, too. It looks a lot like Mrs. Finkleman's pup, Mr. Sixpence. I'd know. I taped up over two hundred "Lost Dog" posters with Mr. Sixpence's photograph last week.

"Hey!" I shout when I recognize the dog's green rhinestone collar. "That *is* Mr. Sixpence! You . . . you can't just go around taking other people's stuff! Or other people's *pets*!"

The Knave descends slowly from his platform of textbooks, stepping menacingly from *Earth Science Today* to *What in the World History?* to *Traditional Language Arts for the Modern Seventh Grader*. Each of his steps is punctuated by another strident honk from the stolen goose.

"*'Can't just go around taking other people's stuff?'*" he repeats, lashing each word with the whip of exaggerated diction. "Haven't you ever heard of 'finders keepers'? If people want to keep their belongings, they should hold on tighter to the things they own. Besides, you know what they say"—he smiles wickedly as, in one smooth movement, he

197

pulls a golden sword from the mountain of objects closest to him—"if you're going to be bad . . . *be horrid.*" He arches his eyebrows as he points the sword at me.

Come on! Really? *This* dude gets to have a totally boss, downright bomb-diggity sword? The bad guy?

I feel myself deflate, but only for a moment. "Give me that dog, Knave! *And* the goose!" Getting ready for action, I begin to unwind the enormous bag from around my neck and shoulders.

"Or you'll do what?" The Knave laughs. "Smother me in burlap?"

"No, I'll give you a few things of mine!" Reordering the alphabet as fast as I can, I point the mouth of my bag in the Knave's direction and shout, "RETAW!"

Water gushes from the bag. The full force of a rushing river knocks the blade out of the Knave's hand. Keeping my aim steady, I zigzag past him as he splutters, spits, and cries out. Water blasts my foe with the power of a fire hose, and the kid struggles for a moment to keep his fancy pants on. Before he hikes them up, I catch a glimpse of the big red hearts printed on his boxers.

As the last of the water drips from the shrinking bag, I head straight toward Mr. Sixpence. But I can't afford to give the Knave any time to recover. As soon as the water runs out, I yell, "SENOTS!" and "SKCITS!" and am propelled backward by the force of all the sticks and stones I collected on my journey. Big stones, small stones, fat sticks, skinny sticks—they all cannon out of the bag in the Knave's direction. I think about calling out the pinecones, too, but I can't figure out how to say "pinecones" backward fast enough.

The Knave is able to weave and dodge enough to avoid the bigger stones, but he doesn't have the same kind of zip and backpedal I've learned during my years of playing dodgeball with Cameron Jamison, so many of the smaller sticks and stones still hit him—though, none very hard. This is good because I'm trying to slow the Knave down, not break his bones.

I reach Mr. Sixpence, but before I pick him up, I launch the biggest, baddest weapon I've collected in my magic-bag arsenal so far. This is an easy one, because it's spelled the same no matter how you say it. Backward or forward, it makes no difference.

I suck in my breath and holler with all my might: "POOOOOP!!!!"

Manure sludges from the bag. It flies in great gloppy, smelly arcs toward the Knave, who doesn't understand what's coming at him until he's buried up to his ears in pig poo. It took me a while, back on that farm, to use my pie pan as a shovel and scoop *this* much manure into my bag, but I had a feeling it would be worth it in the end.

I was right.

I can't resist taking a moment to celebrate my victory in classic Wendell James MacDougall-Flowers style. Never has anyone danced the funky chicken with as much enthusiasm as I do now.

The Knave shouts curses at me as I tuck the shrunken burlap bag under one arm and Mrs. Finkleman's dog under the other. His curses follow me as I run farther into the labyrinth of stolen junk, guided by the thunderous sound of honking.

I find the goose in the far corner of the warehouse, in what can only be described as a jail cell. A *supersize* jail cell. But it isn't the size of the massive cage that brings me skidding to a halt. It is the size of the goose. Even Mr. Sixpence finds the sight of the goose alarming; he whines and wiggles in my arms, trying to climb over my shoulder. When the goose honks again, the sound vibrates my entire body. I suppose that's what happens when a waterfowl the size of a minivan decides to make some noise.

"What the flippin' flapjacks?" I whisper to the dog. It's no wonder Mother is so keen to get her goose back. *This* particular goose may indeed be cooler than a Nintendo 3DS after all.

I shake my head in awe; the bird is practically big enough to ride. In fact, when I look closer, I see that Mother's goose has already been outfitted with a saddle. A *saddle*. At first, I can't believe it. Then I remember that not one thing has been believable since the moment Cameron stuffed me into Allie's locker. Better to just roll with it.

Somewhere behind me, the Knave roars in fury. I get the sinking feeling that he's freed himself from my massive manure bomb and is coming after me, now a Super Angry Triple-Rotten Villain Deluxe.

I can think of only one thing to do.

"Hang on, Mr. Sixpence," I say, tightening my grip on Mrs. Finkleman's dog. "You and I are going for a ride."

I unlatch the door of the cage and let it swing open. Murmuring what I hope are soothing, goosey sounds, I step inside. The giant goose raises its head and beats its enormous wings. It's a threatening gesture, and an impressive sight.

"I'm here to free you, goose," I say, raising my free hand in a placating gesture. "I'm here to bring you back to Mother. She sent me here to get you."

This seems to do the trick. The goose cocks its head at

the name "Mother." Then it folds its wings, ruffles its feathers, and sits. When I continue to stand rooted in place, the goose reaches out with its beak and half steers, half shoves me and Mr. Sixpence toward its saddle.

I am only partially settled atop the goose when the Knave charges into the cage, covered in muck and reeking to high heaven. If he'd been thinking more clearly, he could've easily trapped me by simply slamming the door closed and latching it from the outside. But it's probably hard to think clearly when you're covered in manure, so instead he charges toward me like a poopy, mindless missile.

The goose stands quickly and rears back again, sending me tumbling over its tail into the straw. Mr. Sixpence snaps and growls at the Knave from up above, where he has somehow managed to stay fixed among the goose's downy feathers.

With a cry, the Knave comes at me, fist raised and ready. But before he can slam his knuckles into my nose, I open my magic bag and say . . . nothing. Nothing backward. Nothing forward. I simply let the Knave's momentum carry him fist-first—*SHHWWWWIP!*—into the bag, where he promptly disappears. Snip, snap, snout, his tale told out.

The goose appears to know what it's doing and where it wants to go. I cling to the reins, and to Mr. Sixpence, as we travel aloft, flying so high we practically brush cobwebs from the sky. The moon is up, and I swear a cloud that's shaped exactly like a jumping cow passes over it. I blink my eyes. This place is beginning to mess with my mind.

When we land in Mother's garden, the old woman rushes outside to greet us.

"Well, buckle my shoe! You're back sooner than I expected," she says as I climb down from the goose, holding Mr. Sixpence and trying to brush straw from the goose cage out of my hair.

Mother reaches out and scratches Mr. Sixpence under the chin. "I see you've found even more than what you came here looking for, young Wendell." The pup doesn't bark. Instead, he turns his face toward mine and licks my chin. I'm not entirely sure what Mother means about finding more than I came looking for. It's not like I came to this world on purpose.

"And the Knave?" Mother lifts her eyebrows, waiting.

"He won't be bothering anyone anymore," I say, and I hand her the burlap bag, which is now Knave-sized in its totally empty proportions. "You can figure out what to do with him now."

"I can indeed." Mother chuckles as she takes the bag and begins to fold it. "Now, I believe it's half past time to send you home, young man. But first you must kneel so that I may bestow on you one final gift, something you can carry with you. Something that will remind you of what you are capable of achieving."

My heart begins to play pat-a-cake with my rib cage and I think, *This is it! This is the moment I get my* true *weapon, at last. My Sword of Whatsit. My Hammer of Whosit!*

Whiffling my lips madly from side to side, I kneel in the old lady's radishes, trying to look dignified.

I hold out my hands and close my eyes. I feel cold metal touch my palms. The cold metal of . . .

A shiny new pie pan.

And somehow it feels exactly right.

I spill from Allie's locker and land on the floor of the seventh-grade hallway, clutching my pie pan and holding Mr. Sixpence safely in my arms. Won't Mrs. Finkleman be glad to have her pup back!

Time must work differently in Mother's world. Here, it's no longer nighttime; it's the middle of passing period, and Mr. Sixpence and I narrowly avoid getting trampled by my classmates. Mr. Sixpence starts yapping as soon as the daze of traveling through a crazy, sucking black-hole vacuum-vortex thingy wears off. But the hallway is so noisy—tennis shoes squeaking; locker doors slamming; kids talking, laughing, yelling—no one appears to notice the funny bark of a small dog.

Suddenly, one voice rises to the top.

Allie Chen is shouting. Her voice rings with authority, even if she is only twelve years old, like me.

"You give that to me right now, Cameron! That 3DS belongs to Wendell. It's even got his name on it. You can't go around taking other people's stuff!"

I jolt upright and look around for Allie. She's standing a short way off, surrounded by Cameron Jamison and his friends. She jumps again and again as she tries to grab my 3DS, which Cameron is holding high above his head. Her canvas tote bag sits forgotten on the floor nearby. It has a pig on it, which makes me smile.

"Back off, Chen!" Cameron laughs as Allie makes another valiant leap for my handheld game system. "Haven't you heard of 'finders keepers'? It's not my fault I just happened to find this in Wendell's hands. If he wanted it so badly, he shouldn't have let me take it from him."

Cameron's little speech gives me an uncomfortable feeling of déjà vu. Didn't the Knave say something similar less than forty minutes ago, back in the world I'd just come from?

For a moment, I silently will Allie to cease and desist. No one has ever stood up for me the way she's doing, but I don't want her to risk life and limb or have other kids laugh at her for going up against Cameron on my behalf. Our fellow seventh graders have become spectators in the hallway, watching Allie fight for what's right, all by herself. Even Jay Gupta is here, acting like he doesn't care one way or another that Cameron stole my 3DS. Acting like he doesn't care one way or another that Allie might be about to get stuffed inside someone else's locker before the next bell rings.

I straighten up. I hold my arms still and ready at my sides, but I can't help bouncing on my toes a little. I no longer have the burlap bag or the shepherd's crook, but I do have my shiny new pie pan. And some shiny new confidence.

I went up against the Knave. The *Knave*. If I could stand up to that guy, I'm pretty sure I can stand up to a punk like Cameron Jamison. Especially since, this time, I won't be alone.

"You heard what Allie said, Cameron," I call out, making heads turn up and down the hallway. "You can't go around taking other people's stuff!" I put down Mr. Sixpence and stride over to stand next to Allie. She glances my way, then does a double take. Her gaze jumps quickly from the bump on my forehead to the straw in my hair before settling at last on the pie pan in my hand. Her eyes widen in surprise, then in dawning comprehension. I can see from her expression that she knows *exactly* where I've been.

Giving me a crooked smile, Allie reaches down, dips one hand into her tote bag, and pulls out a shiny metal pie pan, just like mine.

She nods at me. I nod back. Champion greeting champion. Together, we stand up to Cameron Jamison as a pair of true Grandville Middle School *Warriors*. Ready to help out when help is needed.

Ready to be heroes.

THE HERO OF THE STORY

BY LEMONY SNICKET

Years and years ago, when I was about your age, I found myself alone in a park in winter without a coat on a terrible afternoon. My story doesn't begin there, of course. I wasn't born in the park. But this story takes place during a time when I was frightened of a baby, and it ends the next morning, shortly after sunrise, when I stopped being frightened, and it begins on a particular park bench.

Before this story begins, I was frightened of many other things, and I was thinking about those things when the woman approached me. I was frightened that I had nowhere to live. I was frightened that I had nothing to eat. And I was frightened that it was very cold outside and that I had no coat. As I said, it was a terrible afternoon, and I had been having a number of terrible afternoons, and nights and mornings, too, all in a row, like the cars of a train, and me sitting there wishing each car passing in front of me was the caboose. I had been utterly unsupervised for a number of months, for reasons that have nothing to do with this story, a situation that was often frightening. To make myself feel better, I had gotten into the habit of thinking about myself as a hero, like a young man in a fairy tale, alone on a journey to seek my fortune. So far everything had proven more difficult than it was in those stories. I had not found a princess who never laughed, or a talking goose who could turn grain into gold, or an enchanted briefcase, or anything else that would allow me, the hero, to find my fortune and live happily in some faraway realm. I was in a large city stuffed with gray brick buildings, and no one had need of a thirteen-year-old boy all alone. A shopkeeper had offered me a job sweeping the sidewalk, but then said I hadn't done it well enough and took her broom back. A cook had hired me to scrub pots, but the soap was slippery, and I dropped a pot on his foot, and he threw me out of the yam-and-noodle restaurant without letting me take my coat off its hook, so I didn't even have the few coins in my coat pocket, which I needed in order to stay one more night in an old and dirty room down by the docks. I tried to think how else a thirteen-year-old boy could earn those coins, but all I could think of was babysitting, and I didn't know anyone with a baby. Truthfully, I didn't think I'd be much of a babysitter, anyway. I wasn't particularly fond of most babies, and I was so cold and miserable, it was clear I wasn't very good at taking care of myself, never mind an infant.

It surprised me, then, that the woman with the baby had the idea to approach me, as I sat there on the bench, shuffling my feet a little, shivering and coatless and wondering if I was going to freeze to death. The wind tossed some leaves around my ankles and made a rustling noise I could hear even over the crying of a baby.

The crying was coming from a baby carriage, one of those kinds with a large cloth dome over the baby, and four wheels to move it around. The woman was in a warm bundly coat, and both the coat and the carriage had cloudy stains, as if perhaps something had spilled all over them.

"Excuse me," the woman was saying to me. "I've just spilled tea all over, as you can see. Would you watch my baby while I run back to the tea shop and get some paper napkins or a towel? I'll only be a minute."

She was already handing me the baby, which frightened me a little. It was a tiny baby, not very old at all, and it was one of those babies that looks angry, with a mad mouth, little angry tufts of hair, and fierce eyes looking right at me, dead silent, like we were already arguing. It looked like it was in a purple velvet sack, though it was probably a little robe, glittery and fancy, like what a wizard might wear in a story when he arrives to help the hero. There was even a little hat to match, tucked down on the angry baby's head so that just a few tufts, which I've mentioned, stuck out toward me. I didn't want it. I wasn't frightened of the baby like I'd be frightened of a vampire or an avalanche. I was frightened of it like a dark barn, with its creaky door hanging open, or a high staircase, built a long time ago and due to collapse someday soon, perhaps the moment you reach the highest step.

"I'll run and get those napkins for you," I said quickly. I could see the tea shop, which was little more than a shack with a kettle in it, clear across the park, with a few people standing around with steaming clay cups. Maybe if I fetched napkins, I would be considered a hero and given hot tea.

"No, no," the woman insisted, and shoved the baby toward me again so I had to take it. I had to. She began running almost immediately across the park. The baby was warm in my hands, the only warm thing near me, but it was so strangely dressed and angry-looking that I didn't want to hold it any closer. The robe was so thick and soft I couldn't feel the baby's arms anywhere in there, and the idea of an armless baby frightened me so much that I stopped holding the baby and sort of propped it up next to me on the bench. It was a nice bench, wooden but not splintery, and with the baby dressed so fancy it looked a bit like a throne.

"Sit there, Your Highness," I said to the baby, just as a girl went by on a bicycle. She gave me a bit of an odd look but kept pedaling. "Your mother will be right back, Your Highness."

The baby did not relax on the bench. If anything, it looked more cross, and it occurred to me that the woman was not necessarily the baby's mother. Plenty of people hold babies who are not the baby's mother. I was proof of this.

"If she *is* your mother," I added quickly, and to pass the time, and because I was cold, and lonely, I imagined the baby's response.

Of course she's my mother, you fool.

The baby's voice, as I imagined it, was gurgly but clear and sounded neither like a little boy nor a little girl. It just sounded like a baby. "'Fool'?" I repeated. "Why are you calling me names?"

Because I am obviously a fancy and important baby, the hero of the story, and you are just a boy on a park bench.

"Even if that's true," I said, "it's not very nice. After all, I volunteered to take care of you."

You didn't volunteer, the baby didn't say. *You were practically forced. And you're not really taking care of me. I'm just propped up on a bench next to you.*

"Well, if I needed to take care of you, I'm sure I could," I said.

What makes you so sure? And where is my mother, by the way?

This was a good question that I'd imagined the baby asking me. I looked across the park, and neither she nor her baby carriage were anywhere to be seen. The tea shop was still there, with steam from the kettle prowling through the air, but the last customers were leaving, and none of them were the baby's mother. They were all men, for instance. I looked all around, from my seat at the bench, and there was no woman, no baby carriage—no one at all.

I stood up, frightened. My heart, beating, was a little frightened, too. I turned all the way around, twice, looking foolish but feeling close to panic. The woman was nowhere I could see. The baby was still there, though, and it still looked angry.

You can't just leave me on this bench.

"I know," I said, and picked up the baby. It was still warm, and I held it close as I walked to the tea shop, wondering what I should be doing at this point in the story and whether I was the hero or the baby was.

Inside the shack, the teaman was rinsing out a stack of clay cups.

"Excuse me," I said. "Have you seen a woman with a baby carriage?"

"No one's around," the teaman said a little crossly. "I'm closing up."

"A woman spilled tea," I said, "and I've been holding her baby so she could get paper napkins or a towel."

"That's nice of you," the teaman said, and put the cups on a rack to dry. The woman, I thought suddenly, had been holding a baby, but not a cup. What had happened to it, after she'd spilled her tea?

"She never came back," I said.

"Sorry to hear it," the man said.

"We need to find her," I said. "This is her baby."

By now the man was closing the door of the shack and locking it so he could go home. He was not very interested in my story. "You seem a little young to be babysitting," he said.

"I'm not young," I said, "and I'm not a babysitter. I need help finding this woman."

The teaman shrugged into his coat. "If you want to call the police," he said, "go right ahead. I'm not stopping you."

"You're not helping me, either," I pointed out. I had to raise my voice because he was already walking away, putting his key into his pocket. "This is your opportunity to be a hero!" I called after him, but by then, he was gone and once more I could not think what to do. There was no one in the park to help me and no way of fetching the police. I could walk to a police station, but I would have to either take the baby with me, so it would be gone if the woman returned, or leave it there, where who-knows-what could happen. Either way these did not seem like things a hero would do. They seemed like the actions of a villain.

So instead, I sat back down, on another bench, for at least an hour, with the baby on my lap like a bag of groceries that was beginning to fuss. I suppose I could not blame it. The baby had been quiet the whole time it was under my care. *Enough is enough,* I imagined the baby saying, although it was just making little noises, like it was planning on crying soon. I made a short list of things a baby might need, but of course I had none of them. I had no food or a bottle of milk. I had no blankets or toys. I had no mother or father. Something else occurred to me, and I remembered something I'd read recently, that in some places in the world, babies wore leaves instead of diapers. I did not think that picking up some of the rustling leaves and sticking them on the baby was something a hero would do, but thinking about reading gave me the idea to go to the library. I knew right where it was. On other terrible days, I had spent many hours there. Reading at the tables with me were other people without coins or coats who were grateful for the warmth and the shelter, at least until the library closed. It was a good place to go when you didn't know where to go. The library opened promptly each morning at sunrise, but I could not remember if this was one of the days the library stayed open late. I hoped it was. I walked quickly out of the park, carrying the baby as normally as I could, so as not to attract attention, scanning the sidewalks and the pedestrians. Everyone hurried by, but none of them was the woman and her baby carriage.

The library was open, but the librarian behind the desk was the wrong one. Practically every library has one terrific librarian who will help you, and the other one. It was the other one at the desk, so I didn't even bother telling her this story or asking her for advice. I just walked to my favorite part of the shelves, grabbing a book as I went by, and found one of my usual seats by the window. The library windows had thick metal rods between the panes of glass, and I imagined that to the pedestrians outside, it must have looked a little like the baby and me were behind bars. We must have looked like we were in jail together.

I didn't really read to the baby. I read to myself. But I murmured the words out loud as I read them, and the baby stopped fussing, maybe because it was warm, or my voice was soothing, or even because it somehow understood the story and liked it.

The book was a book of stories, one that the helpful librarian had suggested to me a few days ago. She always had good books to suggest to me, even though she had no children herself. She eventually had one, but that's another story. These stories were from all over the world. The one I was reading was from a part of the world where people your age, living in small villages, had to go on a journey and perform an impressive task, after which they would be welcomed back into the village as a hero. In this story the hero was a girl who had decided to slay a giant crab that lived in a cave a few kilometers outside the village. The crab regularly menaced the village—"menaced," I explained to the baby, was a word that here means "attacked people and destroyed things"—and the entire town was desperate.

Surely whoever slew the crab would be considered one of the greatest heroes the village had ever produced.

Surely, the baby agreed, or so I imagined. It startled me out of the story a bit, and I looked around the library for a moment, frightened once more of this baby and wondering what was going to happen. I turned the page and kept reading.

The young girl, whose name was Rona, hatched a plan. First, she found a long vine and stretched it out between two trees, just a few centimeters off the ground. The trees were growing up on the edge of a high cliff, and below the cliff was the churning sea, where Rona thought the crab belonged. Once her trap was set, she journeyed out to the cave where the crab lived and threw sticks into the mouth of the cave until the terrible creature was awake and angry. Clattering over rocks, the crab chased Rona as she ran toward the two trees at the edge of the cliff. The crab was gaining on Rona, closer and closer—and when I read this part, I held the baby closer to me, so it would not be frightened—and several times Rona thought she might stumble and be pinched to death. But she managed to elude the crab and ran to the edge of the cliff with it just behind her, clawing at her heels. She leaped off the cliff, grabbing on to the vine so she would not fall into the sea, and the crab ran right after her without looking carefully, and as the book put it, was suspended in the sky, its many legs and claws all wiggling upward, so for a moment, it looked like a castle in the air, before it fell with an enormous cannonball splash. Rona managed to climb back up the cliff, grinning with pride over her accomplishment, and ran back to tell the village what had happened, and when she told them, they threw a party in her honor and called her a hero.

You might have thought that this was the end of the story. I would have been happy to end it there, now that the baby was quiet and warm in my arms. It seemed happy, and that made me happy, too. But not long after, the emperor came to town with his enormous retinue, which I explained to the baby was a word for advisers and guards and slaves who were carrying the emperor's vast treasure. The emperor had taken an interest in amazing creatures and had heard a rumor about a large crab that lived near the village. He was prepared to offer a great heap of jewels and other valuables if they helped capture the crab for his collection.

Well, of course, the village no longer had a crab nearby, but the villagers were so greedy and eager to get their hands on the treasure that they offered the emperor something else instead: a young and beautiful bride. This, of course, was Rona, but Rona was not interested in marrying the emperor. For one thing, she didn't know him very well. She had never even seem him until he had come to town, for although the village had a statue of the emperor, the crab had clawed it up so much over the years that it looked more like a chubby flagpole than a person. But mostly, Rona was not interested in getting married at all, at least not right then, to the emperor or anyone else. She was only thirteen, after all, and fresh from her hero-making adventure. She wanted to see what would happen next.

Despite her protestations, Rona was packed up immediately and taken by the emperor's retinue to the palace and married to him in a matter of days, while the villagers celebrated with the heap of jewels the emperor had left behind as a reward—or perhaps "payment" was the better word, I murmured to the baby—for this young and beautiful bride. She had to marry him. She had to.

Life with the emperor was even more unpleasant than Rona had anticipated. The emperor was very loud and boring, and he already had a whole pack of wives who had turned into very boring people themselves, probably from being holed up in the emperor's palace for so long. Rona couldn't stand it. She asked again and again to go home, but the emperor, seeming to hardly listen to her, again and again refused.

One afternoon, wandering miserably around the palace, she found the answer to her problems: a long bell pull, which is a cord attached to a bell to ring for servants or snacks. It was thin and stretched easily and reminded Rona of the vine that had made her a hero. That night, while everyone in the palace was very asleep, she took the bell pull and stretched it out between two lamps as tall as trees, and right then, a noise startled me out of the book, and I looked up at a man standing outside the library window, pointing at me and shouting. Through the thick glass I could not hear what it was he was shouting, but in moments he had hurried into the library to keep shouting at me. His loud and panicky voice was such a shock in the library, where, of course, it was supposed to be quiet, that at first I could not hear exactly what it was the man was saying, particularly once the baby started wailing. This upset me, and by the time the police arrived, it was hysterical.

I was not handcuffed at the police station, but I was placed in a room with one tiny window, way up top near the ceiling, and a heavy table with uncomfortable chairs and a door they slammed so loudly I did not even get up to check if it was locked. That was as good as handcuffs at keeping me still. I sat in the room for a little while with my heart pounding. The police had taken the baby away, of course, and my arms did not know what to do with themselves after holding it for so long. Even so, I was still frightened of the baby. I was no longer frightened about what might happen to it. I was frightened about what might happen to me because it had fallen into my care.

Sure enough, when the police inspector came in—tall and cross-looking, with her hair in one long braid down her back—the first thing she said to me was "You're in a heap of trouble."

"I know it."

"Tell me your name."

"Lemony Snicket," I said, although I'd already told her my name, just as I'd told the shouting man and the wrong librarian and the other police officers, the ones who'd arrested me.

"Why did you steal a baby, Lemony Snicket?"

"I didn't steal it. I told you this. Someone asked me to watch their baby."

The inspector sat down across from me with her hands folded. In the pocket of her uniform was a small handsome notebook and a skinny pen, but she didn't take them out, as if my story were so false and useless there was no sense writing it down. "You're a villain, do you know that,

Snicket? Only a villain takes a baby that does not belong to him."

"A woman asked me to take care of it."

"So you say. What did this woman look like?"

"I told you this already. I told you the whole story."

"Tell me again."

"Just a woman. She had stains on her coat, and she was pushing a baby carriage. She asked me to hold her baby while she went to get napkins or a towel."

"Do you know, Lemony Snicket, that two police officers went to the home of the man who runs the tea shop at that particular park? And that the man remembers no such woman? He remembers you well enough, though. He told us that you told him you weren't a babysitter."

"I'm not," I said. "I was just watching the baby for a minute, because the woman asked me to. But then she never came back."

"Are you trying to tell me you're a hero? Because a hero wouldn't have hid in the library with his face behind a book. A hero would have recognized this very important baby and made sure he was returned safely."

"Important?" I asked.

"*Very* important," the police inspector said, but I didn't understand. In one sense, of course, all babies are important, at least to somebody. But no particular baby is really more important than any of the other babies, so I didn't know what the inspector meant until she told me.

"That baby," she said, "is the emperor of Cramiton."

I blinked back at her.

"'Emperor' means 'king.'"

"I know what the word means," I said, "but I don't know what you're talking about."

"The baby is the emperor of Cramiton," the inspector repeated. "It's a tiny region some kilometers away. He won't be crowned until he turns thirteen, but in the meantime he's being cared for in a wonderful palace. A few days ago he went missing. His photograph was in all the newspapers, with an enormous reward for his safe return."

"I haven't purchased a newspaper recently," I said, thinking of the coins in my coat pocket.

"Well, you *should*," the inspector said crossly. "A child in danger is a terrifying emergency, although you're probably too young to understand that. Lucky for you, while you were hiding the emperor in the library, a man happened by and spotted you both through the window. He recognized the emperor immediately and will soon receive the reward. He's a hero, Lemony Snicket, whereas you are a kidnapper and a villain, and you'll be behind bars by sunrise."

"But I had no idea who the baby was," I said. "The woman just handed it to me."

The inspector smiled then, but it was a sharp smile, the kind an alligator must have when a swimmer gets into the water. "You were heard," she said triumphantly, "calling the baby 'Your Highness.' The police commissioner's daughter was bicycling through the park and heard you with her own recently pierced ears. She told her mother all about it as soon as she got home, so the police were already looking for you when that hero spotted you in the library. She's a hero, too, that brave and observant girl."

"I just called the baby 'Your Highness' because of the way it was dressed."

The inspector stood up. "*He* is dressed that way," she said, emphasizing "he" to tell me how wrong I was, "because he is the emperor. Stay here, Snicket, until the jailer arrives to take you away."

She marched out of the room, clattering the door shut behind her. I heard her footsteps as she tramped down the hall, and I sighed in my seat. In many ways I felt the same as I did at the beginning of this story, on the bench in the park. I was frightened about what would happen to me, and once again I could not figure out what to do. I wondered if Rona would know.

I have troubles of my own, I imagined her saying. Her voice was less gurgly than I had imagined the baby's.

"I know," I replied. "Right before that man started shouting at me, it seemed like you were about to trick the emperor to his death, just as you did with the giant crab."

What's wrong with that? she asked me in the empty room. It must have been late at night by now. The tiny window was just a deep black square, a moonless night sky.

"Well," I said, "killing a menacing crab made you a hero. But killing your husband, even if he's boring and you never wanted to marry him, seems like something else."

You think I'm a villain?

"You could run away," I said, "instead of killing the emperor."

You could have gone to the police, Rona did not point out, *instead of the library. Maybe you're the villain, Lemony Snicket.*

"Maybe I am," I said miserably. "Everybody certainly seems to think so."

Everyone thought I was a hero, Rona said imaginarily, *until the emperor came to town.*

"Our stories are very similar," I said.

I pictured Rona shrugging at me. There had been an illustration of her in the library book, a fierce-looking girl with short hair and glasses that made her eyes look even sharper, so I could easily picture her thoughtful shrug. *The trouble is,* I imagined her saying, *my story's in a book, and yours is right here in the world.*

I shrugged back at her, but my shrug was sadder. She was right, so I cut short our imaginary conversation and lay my head down on the table. I lay there for quite some time. It did not make for a comfortable pillow, but it was more comfortable than I'd expected to find that night. The library was long closed by now, and the park, dark and dangerous. The shopkeeper was probably home in bed, and the cook had likely closed up his restaurant without even noticing my coat, which I knew I would never see again. The police commissioner's daughter was probably asleep with a smile on her face, having been called a hero just for seeing me in the park, and the man who had seen me through the window was probably celebrating his reward, and hopefully someone was taking proper care of the baby emperor. I did not know where the woman was, the woman who had given me the baby and the heap of trouble I was in. I tried to imagine, but I could only picture her in the park, pushing the baby carriage away from me, with the sound of crying fading away, and this made me sit up straight. I could not tell how long I had been asleep, but I was wide-awake now. I had figured something out. It made me feel less like a villain the more I sat and thought about it.

The crying was coming from inside the baby carriage. But the baby the woman handed me was silent and staring. There were two babies. I didn't know what it meant, but it was something to think about, a story more interesting than my own miserable one.

The police inspector came back while I was still thinking. She had something with her, and I saw almost immediately it was the baby in its purple robe. The hat was gone, and it was not difficult to see why. The police inspector was being very careless with the baby, plunking it down on the table right in front of me even though it could not sit up by itself. It began to topple almost immediately, so I reached out to steady the baby and then put it in my lap for safekeeping, although I was surprised the inspector would let me touch the baby if it was supposed to be so important. She cleared that all up at once.

"*This,*" she said, flicking one hand out to gesture at the baby, "is *not* the emperor."

I looked at the baby in my lap. It looked back at me crossly. *What do you want?*

"We checked," the inspector said. "It has a similar face

and the same hair. It's wearing the emperor's clothes. But it's not the emperor." She sat down sternly and fiddled with her braid. "It's a girl, for instance," she said, and then stared so hard at me that I knew it was my turn to talk.

"Are you sure?" I asked.

The inspector snorted rudely. "Am I sure it's a girl?"

"Are you sure about all of it?"

"Sure I'm sure."

"So I'm not in a heap of trouble anymore?"

"I guess not," she said. "And that man won't be getting a reward."

"So he's not a hero anymore?"

"That's beside the point," the inspector said, using a phrase that here means she didn't want to talk about it with me. "The real emperor is still missing. And, of course, we've got to look for this woman you told us about and give her back this baby."

"Weren't you looking for her already?"

"No," the inspector admitted sourly. "We thought you were a villain so we didn't believe a word you said. Do me a favor, Snicket, and watch this baby for a minute while we look for its mother."

"*Her* mother," I said, but the inspector had already stalked out the door, not even bothering to close it all the way, the way she had when I was still a villain. I was alone with this baby, for the second time in just a few hours. "Well, Your Highness," I said to the baby, "I guess I'm not a villain anymore."

I guess not, the baby agreed in my imagination. *And you don't have to call me "Your Highness."*

"But I like calling you 'Your Highness,' Your Highness."

Someone might hear you, the baby didn't say, *and you'd be in trouble all over again.*

"I wonder if the commissioner's daughter is still a hero," I said, thinking of the girl on the bicycle.

She didn't really do anything wrong, the baby said.

"Neither did I," I said.

Well, you could have taken me to the police instead of going to the library.

"You ended up with the police, anyway," I pointed out, "and they weren't helpful."

Well, they're going to find my mother.

"Your mother," I said, "if she really is your mother, is a kidnapper. She had the real emperor in her baby carriage and dressed you in his clothing. She left you with me to throw the police off her trail."

Is that true?

I blinked at the baby. "Yes," I said, "but I didn't figure it out until I explained it to you."

Am I a hero for helping you figure it out?

"Maybe," I said, "and maybe I'm a hero for what I'm doing now."

Why are we leaving? Where are we going?

"I'm not going to have the police place you in the care of a kidnapper," I whispered to the baby as I walked quietly out of the police station. Nobody took much notice of me, now that I wasn't a villain.

If you take me with you, aren't you a kidnapper yourself?

"I don't know," I said once I was outside. It was chilly out, and I held the baby as close as a coat as I began to walk. "Rona, what do you think?"

Rona shrugged thoughtfully again, at least in my mind. *Some people will think you're a hero, and some people will think you're a villain.*

"You could say that about anyone," I said.

Does it matter what people say? Or is it more important what you think of your own actions?

I wasn't sure if the baby said this, or Rona, even though, of course, I was sure nobody had said it, and none of us said anything more until I walked up the library steps. It was sunrise, and the place was just opening. The good librarian was there, unlocking the door and watching me approach with the baby, and I guess you know the rest of the story, because as I'm sure you've guessed by now, the baby was you, and now you're around thirteen, just the age I was when you were left with me in the park. You know that the real emperor was found, just a few days later, and that the woman was sent to jail for kidnapping and that she never mentioned you, to the police or to anyone else. Maybe she knew you were being raised by a kindly librarian and didn't want the police interfering, or maybe she was too selfish to even think of you. Maybe she wasn't your mother after all, and you were yet another baby she'd kidnapped. In any case she seems pretty villainous, although the librarian seems to have been a kindly mother to you, so maybe the woman was a hero for helping you get raised by someone so kind. I'm sure I don't know. I moved out of that city that very afternoon, for reasons that have nothing to do with this story, and so I haven't seen you since that day, although I hear you are an interesting and curious person. Certainly you have had an interesting and curious childhood, and you are the hero of that childhood and of your own story. I don't know what I am in this story. It's hard enough to decide what I am—hero or villain or something else—in my own story, let alone yours. Besides, you can decide for yourself, just as I decided things for myself and just as Rona did, in that other story I read to you so long ago. I wish we hadn't been interrupted on that terrible night. As with all good stories, I would have liked to know what happened next.

How My Mother Was Arrested for Murder
BY JACK GANTOS

The old Florida bungalow kept stinking of cooking gas. Dad had checked the pilot lights on the stove, and the pipe connections running from the stove to the big silver gas tank out back. But he could not locate a leak. We sniffed around the kitchen like bloodhounds, but only found decaying bugs, mold in the corners, and bits of cruddy food that had been left behind by a hundred years of renters. After our sniffing, all we could agree upon was that the smell was stronger in the afternoon.

One evening it was especially bad, and Mom was worried that if Dad lit a cigarette, the house would explode like a bomb, so she made him smoke and drink his beer out on the front porch while she opened the windows and turned on all the ceiling fans. He grumbled about being sent outside, but he went, which to me meant that he thought there was something seriously wrong. I needed some fresh air so I joined him.

Dad sat quietly in a wicker porch chair and blew smoke rings up toward the ceiling light fixture. When he finished his beer he said, "Listen up. I have a few thoughts to share."

I looked toward him like a loyal dog.

"A house filled with gas," he began, "can be set off in a lot of ways. You don't need a match to blow up this place. The way it happens is simple. Suppose the house is filled with gas, and you come home from school. What's the first thing you do?"

I tried hard to come up with the right answer. "When I come home," I answered carefully, "I open the door."

Dad nodded. "What's the next thing you do?"

"I turn on the lights," I replied.

"And next?"

"I walk down to the kitchen."

"Next?"

"I turn on the radio."

Dad leaned forward and dropped his cigarette into his

empty beer can and shook it around. "You'd be dead at least three different times," he said, holding up three fingers. "First, as soon as you turn on the lights, the spark from the switch would set the place off. *Kaboom!* But let's say you didn't turn on the lights. So, you walk down the hall. The little metal cleats or nails on the bottoms of your shoes might give off a spark on the tile floor, and *kaboom*! You are dead again. But let's say you were wearing sneakers. Then when you turned on the radio, *kaboom*! Switching on any electrical appliance gives off a spark, and you are burned toast."

"Can I use a flashlight?" I asked. I wanted to read at night without blowing myself up.

"Yeah, a flashlight is okay," he figured. "Just don't drop it and break the little bulb, because the red-hot filament could set off the gas."

"What if the fillings in my teeth rubbed together in my sleep and made a spark?" I asked in an attempt to make a joke.

"Don't be ridiculous," he snapped. "Honestly, I hope you don't say stupid things like that in public and embarrass yourself."

Somehow I never knew when he would slip out of a good mood and into a bad mood and put me in my place with a harsh remark. He was unpredictable. To end the conversation, he turned his face toward the ceiling and lit another cigarette.

Just then, Mom stepped onto the porch with her hands on her hips and a worried look on her face. She was still dressed in her blue-and-gray bank teller uniform. "This gas problem makes me nervous," she said, "especially with the baby at home, breathing it in all day. I'll have to ask the sitter to make sure he gets lots of fresh air."

"Don't worry," Dad replied. "I'll call the gas company tomorrow and tell them to come out."

I took off my shoes and flipped them over to look for nail heads that might kick off a spark. The gas problem was making us all very edgy.

Mom was the one who solved the mystery. The next day, she came home unexpectedly early from work to wait for the gas inspector. When she walked in through the back kitchen door, she surprised the new babysitter, Missy, who had a grip on the back of the baby's head and was holding his little face down over an unlit gas burner as she sang him a lullaby. It was time for the baby's afternoon nap, and Missy was gassing him to sleep and must have been doing so for the weeks she had been taking care of him.

Mom screamed. Missy jumped back from the stove. "I'm not doin' anything wrong," she squealed. "He's colicky, and a little gas settles him down."

Mom dashed forward and snatched the baby out of her arms. "Wait till my husband gets his hands on you," she said with authority. "He'll have you thrown in jail."

Missy turned and ran out the front door and up the driveway and down the road toward the bus stop.

When we all came home and were gathered around the dinner table, Mom blurted out the whole story about Missy, the baby, and the gas. "I swear," she said in a fury. "If I ever see her again . . . I'll do something drastic."

"What could you do about it?" asked Betsy, my older sister.

My mother paused and gave the question a moment's thought. "I'm not sure what I could do. But I'll tell you this," she replied in a firm voice. "I was so angry, if I'd had a gun, I'd have shot her dead on the spot."

I had never heard my mother say something that violent before, and I didn't know exactly how to feel about it. But since we didn't have a gun in the house, I figured it was just an expression of her anger.

Mom continued. "And who knows, the baby may have brain damage," she said nervously, holding the baby close to her face and kissing his forehead. She gently pressed his little belly, as if he were a squeeze toy, while she sniffed his mouth and nose for any escaping gas.

"Oh, he's okay," Dad remarked, making light of her concern as he lit a cigarette. "He's one of our kids, so he's brain damaged already."

Mom managed a strained smile. "I'll call the doctor," she replied.

"Don't you think we should call the police?" Betsy asked. "I mean, what the sitter did was like a Nazi war crime."

"It would just be your mom's word against hers," Dad replied with a shrug. "But, if anything should be done, I'll take care of it myself. Do you know where she lives?"

Mom pretended not to hear him. I knew she didn't want him to fly off the handle and go to Missy's house and do something he'd regret. "Well," she said calmly, trying to settle things down. "Let's not get mixed up in it. Let's just be happy that we're all fine."

But Dad did not feel fine. The next evening he came home late from work. We were finishing dinner when he sat down and took his place. Mom leaned forward to serve him, but he waved her off. "I ate already," he said, which meant he had gone to his club with his drinking buddies before coming home. Then from the inside pocket of his canvas work jacket, he pulled out a crumpled brown paper bag, which contained something no larger than his hand. He extended his arm across the table and lowered it with a clunk on Mom's dinner plate.

"What's this?" Mom asked.

"A little gift for you," he replied slyly. His eyes were twinkling in the same cheery way they did when he handed out the gifts from under the Christmas tree.

Mom reached into the bag. "Oh my God," she uttered, and when she removed her hand, there was a small revolver in her grip. "What's this for?" she asked, a bit shocked. Her hand was shaking.

"You said," Dad replied smoothly, "that if you had a gun, you would have shot that woman. Well, now you have the correct piece of equipment in your hand, and if that little babysitter issue ever occurs again, you can take care of business."

I stared at the revolver and leaned back in my chair. It scared me to look at it, and when Mom swung it to my side of the table, I ducked down.

"Tell me this is a toy," she said sternly, aiming her words directly at my dad. "Tell me this isn't what I think it is."

"It's just a .25-caliber revolver," he said casually. "A proper lady's model. You can keep it in your purse."

"I'd rather not take the law into our own hands," Betsy said bravely, and shook her head in disapproval. "Remember, those who live by the sword die by the sword."

"I, for one, will sleep a lot easier with a gun in the house," Dad replied, and thumped himself on the chest. "There is a lot of crime out there. Why, just down the street, a guy was stabbed in the leg."

"By his wife," Betsy added, "because she was defending herself."

"Shush, you two," Mom said, and she looked across the table at Dad. "The last thing we need in this house is a handgun. I just don't think they are safe, especially with kids around."

"Believe me," Dad replied, "the only reason to be afraid of a firearm is if you don't know how to use it. Let me give you a shooting lesson," he suggested. "Afterward, I bet you'll feel a lot more comfortable with it. Plus, when I travel for business, I'll always know you have my back and can protect the kids."

"Well, I've never fired a revolver before, just rifles," she said, sounding like she'd give it a chance.

"There's nothing to it," Dad said. "You just point and shoot."

A little later, after the dinner table was cleared, he pulled a box of ammunition out of a bag and sat down with her and showed her how to load the six small bullets into the revolver's cylinder. When the sun went down, he drove her out to the Western Glades horse track. It was a moonless night. The racing season was over, and the track was the biggest stretch of unlit land where Mom could safely shoot.

When she came home, she didn't seem so concerned about having the little revolver in the house.

"How'd it go?" I asked, since she returned in an upbeat mood.

"Not bad," she replied. "I just pointed it out into the night and kept pulling the trigger until it was empty. It was more like firecrackers going off."

"Did you hit anything?" I asked.

"Nah," she replied as she unpinned her hair. "It was too dark."

The next morning I woke up when Mom screamed out, "Oh my God!"

I scrambled out of bed and ran into the hall, where I bumped into Betsy as we raced into the kitchen. Mom was standing with her hands pressed over her mouth. She seemed frozen as she stared at the newspaper, which had dropped to the floor.

Dad was standing behind her with his hands kneading her shoulders. "It means nothing," he insisted. "Nothing."

"*What* means nothing?" Betsy demanded.

Dad nodded toward the newspaper. The headline read, "Man Found Shot Dead at Racetrack."

"But it wasn't her," Dad said. "Couldn't have been."

"Of course it was me," Mom cried out. "I was the only idiot out there in the night, firing off a handgun, and now there is a dead man."

"What if it was her?" Betsy asked. "What would we do?"

"I'm not sure," Dad replied. "Maybe we'd have to sneak her out of the country."

"Have you lost your mind?" Mom asked.

"It was just a suggestion," he replied. "Do you have a better idea?"

"Yes, I do," she replied directly. "I can call the police and tell them that I accidentally shot that poor man."

"What good will that do?" Dad asked. "The guy is dead. The police can't bring him back to life."

Just then, the baby began to cry. Betsy trotted up the hall. When she returned, Mom reached for him.

"Hey, let's get to the real point," Dad continued as he reached down and picked up the newspaper. "Accidental shootings happen all the time. Once," he continued, "on

New Year's Eve, Gooz Youski went out onto his back porch and fired off a clip from his deer rifle. Next day they found an unlucky guy in Hecla shot dead through the head with a deer slug. Same caliber bullet. We figured it was Gooz, but nobody said anything. It was an accident. Nobody could reverse what had happened, so why make it worse by sending Gooz to the slammer? Besides, we were all a little impressed with Gooz, because he had never hit a moving target before in his life." Dad smiled at his attempt to make a joke until he noticed we were all staring back at him as if he were insane.

"Well, I'm no Gooz Youski," Mom countered, growing more indignant. "And I'm not keeping my mouth shut. If I shot that poor man, I'll pay the price. Besides, it's my stupid fault for agreeing to let that gun into this house in the first place. In my gut I knew it would lead to trouble."

"Hey, it's not the gun's fault," Dad quickly replied.

"You're right," Mom snapped back. "It's *my* fault, pure and simple, and now I'm going to try to make up for the mistake by telling the truth." She tightened her arms around the baby and marched down the hall.

Dad raised his voice so she could still hear him. "Well, at best it would just be a manslaughter charge," he hollered.

"You couldn't get much time for an accident—maybe a year or two."

Mom turned and stomped right back. She shifted the baby to one arm and stood nose to nose with Dad. With her free hand she pressed a finger against his chest. I was glad she didn't have her gun just then. "Mister," she said sternly as she gave him a poke. "Someone shot and killed an innocent man, and the evidence points to me. These children," she said, turning toward us, "may lose their mother because she listened to you. Now don't make light of this. It's serious!"

Dad gazed up at the ceiling and waved his hand in front of his face like he was shooing a fly. "No big deal," he maintained. "You're making a mountain out of a molehill. You'll see."

"Indeed we will," Mom snapped. Then she retreated into the bedroom. We could hear her dial the telephone, and then she spoke quietly. When she hung up, Betsy, Dad, and I were still standing in the kitchen, like a stunned display of wax figures from a broken family.

"I just spoke to a detective," she announced down the hallway. "He said he would be right over."

"I wish you wouldn't get mixed up in this," Dad pleaded. "That guy could have been shot by anyone."

"I think not," Mom replied. "But for now, let's all get properly dressed. We don't want to look like a bunch of criminals when the police arrive and reporters take our picture."

We were properly dressed and waiting on the front porch when Dad turned to Mom and asked, "Where is the revolver? The cops will need to examine it."

"I threw it down the old well in the backyard," she said nervously.

"That only makes you look guiltier," he insisted, and pressed his hands over his face in frustration. When he lowered them, his skin was bright red, as if his hands had been hot towels.

"I don't know if I'm guilty," she replied. "I'm scared. I just threw it down the well because I didn't want to see it in the house anymore."

Just then, an unmarked police car pulled into our driveway and came to a stop. A plainclothes detective swung open his door and stepped out. He paused to take a good look at the five of us in our church clothes and then stepped forward.

"Which one of you is Mrs. Gantos?" he asked, although he must have known.

Before Mom could speak, Dad reached out to shake the detective's hand and nervously said, "Heck, she couldn't have shot that man. She can't hit the broad side of a barn from ten feet away."

"I'm Detective Wilton," he said in a humorless voice, "and I'm here to find out if that is true or not."

He then turned to Mom. "Where is the gun?" he asked.

She told him.

"I'll send some men around for it," he said. Then he hooked his arm out, as though he were asking her for a dance. Mom declined his arm. "I'll have to take you down to headquarters," he said politely.

She handed the baby off to Betsy and then leaned forward and gave him a little kiss. She was being brave, but I saw her tears and felt my own gather.

"If you have a lawyer," the detective said to Dad, "you should call him."

Dad nodded to that advice as Mom walked to the detective's car and opened the front door. With one hand she tucked her wide skirt behind her legs and then swung herself into the front passenger seat. Before the detective started the car, she leaned out the window and half shouted, "There is nothing to worry about. I want you kids to clean up your rooms. Do your homework, and if you go out to play, be home in time for dinner."

"Yes, Mom," Betsy and I murmured. We were teetering like bowling pins about to fall over.

"I'll meet you there," Dad called back, and his hand was already fishing in his pocket for his car keys.

About an hour later a car with two uniformed police officers arrived. One of them removed a sledgehammer and an extension pole from the trunk. I showed them where the well was in the backyard. The opening had long ago been capped with a square concrete slab, but there was a crack across the top of it, wide enough to step through if you were not careful, or where you could drop a small handgun. I took a seat on the back porch steps and waited for the surprise they were going to get. When one of them took the sledgehammer and hit the cement slab a tornado of brown bats rose up. The police cried out and shied back, their faces tight with fright. I suppose I should have warned them about the bats, but it felt very good to watch them cower, because at that moment, I imagined the detective was scaring Mom.

The bats quickly disappeared beyond the trees, and the cops laughed at themselves. Soon, they smashed open the hole and lowered the extension pole with a wire basket on the end. After a few scoops through the bottom muck, they pulled up the small revolver and shook it out of the basket and into a plastic bag.

They turned and walked away, smiling and teasing each other like kids with their hands darting to and fro, like vampire bats. I watched them leave and thought of the moment Mom had pulled the revolver out of the paper bag and pointed it across the dining room table. "Nothing but trouble," I said to myself.

Later, Betsy fed and bathed the baby and put him to bed. I ate a sandwich and went to my room. I had homework. I opened a book to read, but thinking about Mom and our family and what might happen to us had me in a knot. I closed the book and just sat there with my elbows on my knees, and my eyes out of focus.

When Betsy and I heard Dad's car pull up the driveway, we ventured out of our rooms and stood in the living room. After he opened the door and saw us, he just shrugged and shook his head back and forth. "For now they've charged her," he said, and bit down on his lip. "I don't have the cash for bail just now, but the lawyer and I will try to get it tomorrow."

He opened the refrigerator and removed a plate of leftovers and a beer. I watched him eat. It was like watching someone feasting on another person's troubles. It probably wasn't nice to think about him that way, but that is how I felt. He was the one who should be charged. He gave her the gun. He took her shooting. He should take the blame.

The next day Betsy stayed home with the baby, and I stayed home just because it seemed impossible to get out of my pajamas or take a shower and get dressed and stand at a bus stop or do anything that now belonged to the life I used to have. There had been a good life with Mom, and now there was going to be a lesser life without her. What was that life going to be like? I drifted aimlessly down to her room and opened her closet door. Her dresses just hung there. They were lifeless without her, and so were we.

When Dad came home after dark, I dashed into the living room to greet him. Across his arm was draped Mom's purse, and in a brown grocery bag, he had her other things. Without thinking I blurted out, "Did they execute her?"

Dad winced. "No," he replied. "They just put her in a jail uniform."

Betsy walked down with the baby in her arms. She was feeding him from a bottle. She didn't raise her voice, but there was a dark look on her face when she said, "Well, I guess this means you still don't have the money to bail her out."

"Not yet," he replied. "But I did talk with her. They are

253

treating her okay. She asked about you kids."

He said other things, but I wasn't listening. I returned to my room and switched off the lights. Somehow the little bit of hope I had was easier to see in the darkness.

That night, Betsy opened my bedroom door and quickly closed it behind herself. "Look," she whispered. "It's clear that Dad's not going to get bail money, and the lawyer can't do anything, so I've been thinking of a plan on how to save Mom—and you can help."

"I'll do anything," I said, jumping at the chance. "Just name it."

"I want you to pick up the phone and call the detective. Tell him you fired the gun. They can't throw a kid in jail."

"That's crazy," I said. "They know it's not me."

"You have to *insist* on it," she replied. "Convince them that *you* did it and Mom is taking the blame for what you did. You can say that."

"I can't," I pleaded.

"Look, you are a kid. They'll just slap you on the wrist and let you go. But they might put Mom away in prison for years, and then what would happen to us?"

"You'd have to be the mother," I replied, "and take care of the baby."

"I'm willing to do my part," she said, "whatever it takes. And now it's time for you to do your part. If you take the blame, then no matter what they do to you, the family will be saved. We'll have Mom and Dad and the baby . . ."

". . . and you," I blurted out. "What about me?"

"This isn't about what happens to *you*," she said directly. "It's about what you can do to save the *family*. Besides, no matter what happens, we'll always be there for you. Like, if you went to a boy's prison, we'd visit you every Sunday."

"I would do anything to save Mom," I replied nervously. "But lying is not what she would want, because she didn't lie to the police, even when she had the chance to."

"Listen to me," she demanded. "Mom called me from jail to check on the baby. And I'm not lying when I say that more than anything in the world, she wants to be home taking care of him. We owe her that much."

"We owe her our promise to always tell the truth," I said right back. "So I won't lie. It's wrong."

She looked me up and down and sneered. "What kind of boy are you? You'd rather let her rot in prison than save her?"

"That's not true," I replied. "Mom wouldn't want me to lie."

"A coward always has an excuse," she shot back. "The

fact is, you won't even help your own mother."

Before I could say any more, the baby began to cry. She shot me a detestable glance and then retreated up the hall.

I stood there, feeling pathetic and cowardly. But I couldn't think of any honest way to help. I knew if I called the police and lied, I would just make it worse. Still, maybe there was something I could do. Maybe I could come up with my own plan to help her and the family. Maybe. But what?

Then, before I could think of a sure-fire plan to spring Mom from prison, the next morning she miraculously showed up. Dad had left for work already, and when I heard a car in the driveway, I looked out the window and saw Mom sitting in the detective's car.

"Betsy," I yelled, and ran to the front porch. "Dad must have found the bail money. The police are here with Mom."

Betsy joined me on the front porch. "I guess Mom took my advice," she said. "When she called from jail to check on the baby, I told her to tell the police that you did it. She must have because now they're releasing her and coming to take you away. You better throw yourself at the detective's feet and beg for mercy."

"Drop dead," I said.

Detective Wilton opened his car door and swiftly walked around the front of the car and opened Mom's door. Betsy ran with the baby to Mom's side, and the detective walked toward me.

Maybe he is going to take me away, I thought. But when he reached me, it was only to shake my hand. "Your mother is no longer charged as a suspect," he said politely. "We tested the gun, and it did not fire the bullet that killed the victim."

"Thank you," I said.

Then he called Mom over. He had one more bit of business. Mom handed me the baby, and the detective reached into his pocket and withdrew a small brown bag. "I'm returning your pistol. Please, don't fire it in public places," he said, reprimanding her.

"Don't worry," she assured him. "It will never be fired again as far as I'm concerned."

As soon as the detective drove away, we went into the house. Mom dashed into the kitchen and began to wash the fingerprint ink off her fingers.

"Hey, Mom," I asked. "What about the dead man? What happened?"

"It was a family quarrel," she replied softly. "It was horrid. He was shot in his own home, with his own gun, and by a member of his own family, who dumped his body out by that racetrack."

"That's awful," I said. "But I'm so glad you are back home."

"Me too," she said. "Still, I can't help but feel sorry for that other family. We dodged a bullet, and they did not."

That was so true.

Once we all settled down, Mom sent Betsy up to the corner store to buy formula for the baby and some snacks for us. "Chocolates," she said. "Everything that is sinful!"

As soon as Betsy was gone, Mom called me into her bedroom. She held out the gun. "We have to throw this away," she said secretively. "Someplace where your dad can't find it."

"Okay," I replied. "But you'll have to drive." Dad had the company truck, and the car was in the garage.

"Honey," she said, and gently touched my face, "I haven't been behind the wheel of a car for years. Me driving is more dangerous than me shooting. Besides, you have to do it alone. Betsy will be back at any minute, and I have to stay with the baby. I'll call a cab."

I didn't want to do it alone, but I didn't want to be spineless, either. I still felt bad because when Mom was taken away, I couldn't think of any way to save her. Now I could do my part for the family and save all of us from having a gun in the house. Still, I was scared. Dad would be worse than the police if he figured out what I was doing.

"Where should I hide it?" I asked.

She opened her wallet and gave me twenty dollars. "You pick a spot," she replied. "But don't tell me where. It will have to be your secret."

I took the cab to the fishing pier, which was on a rocky part of the shore, where no one went swimming. I kept the gun in my jacket pocket and walked out to a corner at the very end. I felt suspicious all over, especially with a few fishermen glancing at me. I could feel how angry Dad would be if he knew what I was up to. Even though he didn't know where I was or what I was doing, I knew he would soon want to know the answer to both those questions. He got upset when he found a tool out of place. He'd definitely be on a rampage when he found his gun missing.

It was cloudy. Seagulls were flapping around. The waves foamed up over the ring of coral reefs to one side. It was now or never. I reached into my pocket and removed the pistol. I leaned back, and in one motion, winged it out there. It hit the blue water and splashed like a fish jumping. I bent down and picked up a broken conch shell and threw that too, then another and another, as though I had been throwing broken shells all along.

"Hey!" one of the fishermen finally called out. "You're scaring the fish."

"Sorry," I said, then I turned and quickly walked back down the pier. Across the street was a hotel, where I caught a cab.

It wasn't long before I was home. I entered through the back door. Mom saw me before I could get to my room. "He'll be home soon," she said, and kissed me on the head, then pushed a handful of candy bars into my jacket pocket. "He'll be mad, but he'll get over it. Don't worry. I'll take care of you."

I nodded. I was scared speechless. Would she take care of me before or after he got to me?

Just then, Dad's tires skidded to a stop as he pulled into the driveway. The car door slammed behind him.

"See," he called out happily when he opened the front door. "I said you couldn't hit the broad side of a barn— much less some guy in the dark."

"Don't make a joke of this," Mom replied. "I'm still shaken."

Dad picked her up by the waist and swung her around. "Let's go celebrate," he said. "We'll drive out to the Lobster Trap for lobsters and a cold beer."

"Oh, that would be lovely," Mom replied. She gave him a long kiss. "I've had a rough few days."

"Then let's get a move on," he cried, and headed for the bedroom. Then he stopped.

"Hey, where's the gun?" he asked. "When I called the detective, he said he gave it back to you."

"I got rid of it," she said. "It was nothing but bad luck, so let's not talk about it anymore."

He laughed like he didn't believe her. "Did you throw it in the well again?"

"You told me I was stupid for doing that the first time," she replied as they walked toward their bedroom. "You'll never find it this time. Never in a million years."

"We'll see," Dad replied, and closed the bedroom door. I couldn't hear any more after that, but I knew I was going to have to get ready for him.

It didn't take long for him to shower, and after he finished dressing, he came into my room. He cocked his shoe on the edge of my desk chair and began to tie the laces. "I think you know where that gun is," he said, and turned his face to look me. I don't know what he saw in my eyes, but in his I could see he knew Mom had gotten to me.

He waited for me to tell him, but I stuck to my plan and kept my mouth shut.

"Your mother will eventually tell me everything," he said, tying the other shoe. "She always does."

"She doesn't know where it is," I replied. Then added, "We're all afraid of it."

"That's nonsense. The gun is to protect us. There's nothing to be afraid of."

Yes, there was. We almost lost Mom. And there was the suffering the dead man's family was enduring.

"You know, I'd like to trust you," he said evenly. "But you're making it hard for me because nobody can trust a liar."

I stood there thinking, *He's taking her to dinner, and I'm taking the blame.* But it was worth it to get the gun out of the house.

"Do you have anything more to say?"

I shook my head no.

He shrugged in return, as if it really didn't matter if he trusted me or not, when trusting a person is one of the things that matters most in life.

He looked in my dresser mirror and adjusted his tie. "I guess you know it disappoints me that you are more like your mother," he finally said, then marched out, with the door slamming behind him.

I flicked off the light. I wasn't disappointed in myself.

After a moment Mom cracked open the door. "Jack," she whispered, in her sneaky voice. "Are you in here?"

I didn't answer. *I did my part*, I thought. *You do yours.*

"Let's go, killer." Dad called to Mom from the living room. "I'm hungry."

Mom continued. "I promise there won't be any more guns," she said, and closed the door.

I stood in the dark and didn't move until I heard the car start. Then I hopped onto the bed and jumped up and down on the mattress. The springs creaked as I got higher and higher. I reached out in the darkness and touched the ceiling with the palms of my hands.

"I'm thirteen years old now," I said. "If I live to be a hundred, that's eighty-seven more years of dodging bullets."

ABOUT
GUYSREAD

It's true: Guys Read about heroes and villains. And you just proved it. (Unless you just opened the book to this page and started reading. In which case, we feel bad for you because you missed some pretty heroic stuff.)

Now what?

Now we keep going—Guys Read keeps working to find good stuff for you to read. You read it and pass it along to other guys. Here's how we can do it:

For more than ten years, Guys Read has been at www.guysread.com, collecting recommendations of what guys really want to read. We have gathered recommendations of thousands of great funny books, scary books, action books, illustrated books, information books, wordless books, sci-fi books, mystery books, and you-name-it books.

So what's your part of the job? Simple: try out some of the suggestions at guysread.com, try some of the other stuff written by the authors in this book, then let us know what you think. Tell us what you like to read. Tell us what you don't like to read. The more you tell us, the more great book recommendations we can collect. It might even help us choose the writers for the next installment of Guys Read.

Thanks for reading.

And thanks for helping Guys Read.

JON SZIESZCKA (editor) has been writing books for children ever since he took time off from his career as an elementary school teacher. He wanted to create funny books that kids would want to read. Once he got going, he never stopped. He is the author of numerous picture books, middle grade series, and even a memoir. From 2007–2010 he served as the first National Ambassador for Children's Literature, appointed by the Library of Congress. Since 2004, Jon has been actively promoting his interest in getting boys to read through his Guys Read initiative and website. Born in Flint, Michigan, he now lives in Brooklyn with his family. Visit him online at www.jsworldwide.com and at www.guysread.com.

SELECTED TITLES

THE STINKY CHEESE MAN AND OTHER FAIRLY STUPID TALES (Illustrated by Lane Smith)

The Time Warp Trio series, including SUMMER READING IS KILLING ME (Illustrated by Lane Smith)

The Frank Einstein series, including FRANK EINSTEIN AND THE ELECTRO-FINGER (Illustrated by Brian Biggs)

LAURIE HALSE ANDERSON ("General Poophead") is a bestselling author who writes for kids of all ages. Known for tackling tough subjects with humor and sensitivity, her work has earned many national and state book awards, as well as international recognition. Her first young adult novel, SPEAK, was a *New York Times* bestseller and a Printz Honor winner. SPEAK is taught at middle schools, high schools, and colleges around the country. Laurie also writes historical fiction; her novel CHAINS was a National Book Award finalist. She lives in northern New York State, where she likes to watch the snow fall as she writes. Visit her online at www.madwomanintheforest.com.

SELECTED TITLES

SPEAK

TWISTED

CHAINS

CATHY CAMPER and **RAÚL THE THIRD** ("The Wager") are the author and illustrator, respectively, of the Lowriders in Space series. Cathy is a writer, artist, and librarian. In addition to graphic novels, she also writes picture books and nonfiction and has written articles and stories for children and adults for several different magazines. You can visit Cathy online at www.cathycamper.com. Raúl the Third teaches illustration at the Museum of Fine Arts and the Institute for Contemporary Arts, both in Boston. He was born in Texas and spent his childhood in both Texas and Mexico. You can find him online at www.raulthethird.com.

SHARON CREECH ("Need That Dog") grew up in a noisy, rowdy family in Ohio (and wrote the book ABSOLUTELY NORMAL CHAOS to tell the story). Another place in her childhood that found new life in her books was a cousin's farm in a small town in Kentucky. It had hills, trees, a swimming hole, a barn, and a hayloft. She and her brothers and cousins would run wild outside all day and spend the evenings on the porch listening to stories. She was once a high school English teacher, where she says she learned "what makes a story interesting and about techniques of plot and characterization and point of view." Visit her online at www.sharoncreech.com.

JACK GANTOS ("How My Mother Was Arrested for Murder") is the celebrated author of DEAD END IN NORVELT, which received the Newbery Medal, and JOEY PIGZA LOSES CONTROL, which received a Newbery Honor. He is also the author of the popular picture books about Rotten Ralph and JACK'S BLACK BOOK, an installment in his acclaimed series of semiautobiographical story collections featuring his alter ego, Jack Henry. His book HOLE IN MY LIFE was a Robert Seibert Honor Book and a Michael L. Printz Honor Book. Jack lives with his family in Boston, Massachusetts. You can read more about him online at www.jackgantos.com.

SELECTED TITLES

The Joey Pigza Series, including JOEY PIGZA SWALLOWED THE KEY

The Jack Henry Series, including JACK ADRIFT: *Fourth Grade Without a Clue*

THE TROUBLE IN ME

WRITING RADAR: *Using Your Journal to Snoop Out and Craft Great Stories*

CHRISTOPHER HEALY ("The Villain's Guide to Being a Hero") always knew he would be a writer. He started out by writing tables of contents when he was a kid (no books, just the tables of contents). When he grew up, he wrote articles for magazines, newspapers, and websites about video games. When he had kids, he started to write articles about them—how they behaved, what their rooms looked like, what books they read, what movies they watched, and more. Finally, he decided to write actual books for them to read. Now he just can't stop. Visit him online at www.christopherhealy.com.

SELECTED TITLES

THE HERO'S GUIDE TO SAVING YOUR KINGDOM

THE HERO'S GUIDE TO STORMING THE CASTLE

THE HERO'S GUIDE TO BEING AN OUTLAW

DEBORAH HOPKINSON ("How I Became Stink Daley") has written more than forty books for young readers, including picture books, middle grade fiction, and non-fiction. Most of her books are about history in one way or another. She loves to make history come alive, often basing her books on oral histories and personal stories that help her readers imagine the place and time about which she's writing. She has won many awards for her books and has said that her favorite of all her books is the award-winning SHUTTING OUT THE SKY: *Life in the Tenements of New York 1880–1924*, which was inspired by her grandmother's experience as an immigrant. Visit her online at www.deborahhopkinson.com.

SELECTED TITLES
COURAGE & DEFIANCE: *Stories of Spies, Saboteurs and Survivors in WWII Denmark*

TITANIC: *Voices from the Disaster*

A BANDIT'S TALE: *The Muddled Misadventures of a Pickpocket*

INGRID LAW ("The Warrior and the Knave") was born on the shores of Lake Champlain, which is rumored to be the home of a prehistoric sea monster called "Champ." From the very start, her life was steeped in the lure of the fantastic, of tall tales and big ideas. Her family moved to Colorado when she was six, and her father taught in a one-room schoolhouse. Visiting the schoolhouse, she discovered that small things and small places can be just as interesting and extraordinary as big noisy ones. Fun fact: her second book, SCUMBLE, is dedicated to an imaginary cat. Her first novel, SAVVY, received a Newbery Honor and a *Boston Globe–Horn Book* Honor. Visit her online at www.ingridlaw.com.

SELECTED TITLES

SAVVY

SCUMBLE

SWITCH

PAM MUÑOZ RYAN ("First Crossing") is a bestselling author who has written more than forty books, including the Newbery Honor Book ECHO, ESPERANZA RISING, RIDING FREEDOM, PAINT THE WIND, THE DREAMER, and BECOMING NAOMI LEÓN. She has received many honors and awards for her work. Pam grew up in Bakersfield, California. She says when she was a kid, she was an "obsessive reader." She began her career as a teacher but eventually decided to try to become a writer, and now forty books later, she can't imagine doing anything else. She is often asked "What is your motivation to write?" and her answer is simple: "I want the reader to turn the page." Visit her online at www.pammunozryan.com.

SELECTED TITLES

ECHO

ESPERANZA RISING

BECOMING NAOMI LEÓN

LEMONY SNICKET ("The Hero of the Story") is the author of far too many books, including the four-volume All the Wrong Questions series and the thirteen-volume A Series of Unfortunate Events. Visit him online at www.lemonysnicket.com.

SELECTED TITLES

LEMONY SNICKET: *The Unauthorized Autobiography*

A Series of Unfortunate Events, including THE BAD BEGINNING

All the Wrong Questions series, including WHY IS THIS NIGHT DIFFERENT FROM ALL OTHER NIGHTS?

EUGENE YELCHIN ("Kalash") grew up in Saint Petersburg, Russia, where he trained as an artist and designed sets and costumes for the theater and ballet. His artwork has appeared in newspapers, magazines, and advertisements. He even drew the first polar bears used in the Coca-Cola commercials. He studied film and has directed commercials and designed characters for animated films. He has also illustrated many children's books. His first novel, BREAKING STALIN'S NOSE, received a Newbery Honor and was named one of the best books of 2011 by *The Horn Book*.

SELECTED TITLES

BREAKING STALIN'S NOSE

THE HAUNTING OF FALCON HOUSE

JEFF STOKELY (illustrator) writes and draws comics, drinks coffee, and eats pizza. He says he sometimes likes to draw pizza. "But I never eat comics. Ever." He is cocreator and artist of *The Spire* (with writer Simon Spurrier) and artist of the series *Six-Gun Gorilla* (also with writer Simon Spurrier). He has done character design for *Max Steel* and *Masters of the Universe* and has done illustration work for companies such as Cryptozoic, Tokyopop, and Udon. Visit him online at www.jeffstokely.com.

SELECTED TITLES

The Spire series (artist and cocreator, with writer Simon Spurrier)

Six-Gun Gorilla series (artist, written by Simon Spurrier)

THE REASON FOR DRAGONS (artist/adapter, written by Chris Northrop)

Jon Scieszka presents
THE GUYS READ LIBRARY
OF GREAT READING

Volume 1

Volume 2

Volume 3

Volume 4

Volume 5

Volume 6

Volume 7

How many have *you* read?

WALDEN POND PRESS™
An Imprint of HarperCollinsPublishers

www.harpercollinschildrens.cc
www.walden.com/boc